Eulalia's House

Eulalia's House

(A casa de Eulália)

Manuel Tiago
(Álvaro Cunhal)

Translated and with a foreword by
Eric A. Gordon

INTERNATIONAL PUBLISHERS
New York

Copyright © Editorial «Avante!», 2021

First English language edition, 2021 by International Publishers Co., Inc. / New York by special arrangement with Editorial Avante!

Translated from the Portuguese by Eric Gordon © 2021

Printed in the United States of America
All rights reserved.

Except for brief passages for review purposes, no part of this book may be reproduced or transmitted in any form or by any means, electronic or mechanical, including photocopying, recording, or via any information storage retrieval system, without permission in writing from the publisher.

Library of Congress Cataloging-in-Publication Data

Names: Tiago, Manuel, author. | Gordon, Eric A., 1945– translator, writer of foreword.
Title: Eulalia's house = (A casa de Eulália) / Manuel Tiago (Álvaro Cunhal) ; translated and with a foreword by Eric A. Gordon.
Other titles: Casa de Eulália. English.
Description: First English language edition. | New York : International Publishers, 2021. | Summary: "This is a story of the Spanish Civil War. As the preeminent place in the world where fascism could be stopped in its tracks, Spain captured the imagination of people all around the globe"— Provided by publisher.
Identifiers: LCCN 2021036065 (print) | LCCN 2021036066 (ebook) | ISBN 9780717808786 (paperback) | ISBN 9780717800001 (ebook)
Subjects: LCSH: Spain—History—Civil War, 1936-1939—Fiction. | Portuguese—Spain—Fiction. | LCGFT: Historical fiction. | Novels.
Classification: LCC PQ9282.I23 C3713 2021 (print) | LCC PQ9282.I23 (ebook) | DDC 869.3/42—dc23
LC record available at https://lccn.loc.gov/2021036065
LC ebook record available at https://lccn.loc.gov/2021036066

ISBN-10: 0-7178-0878-5   ISBN-13: 978-0-7178-0878-6
Typeset by Amnet Systems, Chennai, India

Table of Contents

Frontispiece ii
Chapter I 3
Chapter II 21
Chapter III 33
Chapter IV 49
Chapter V 67
Chapter VI 89
Chapter VII 109
Chapter VIII 125
Author Biography 141
About the Translator 143
Questions to Ponder and Discuss 145

Also available from International Publishers
in its series of fictional works by
Manuel Tiago

Five Days, Five Nights
"devoid of the stilted political speechifying sometimes found in political fiction, the novella manages to capture the complexities, loneliness, and bravery of ordinary people"
(*Monthly Review*)

The Six-Pointed Star
"a breathtaking novel of heartbreaking vignettes"
(*Culture Matters*)

The 3rd Floor
"exciting and suspenseful…I could not put the book down as I read the four stories, each in one sitting. Each of them is a page-turner."
(*People's World*)

Border Crossings
"A work of unique concept and clever prose, richly translated. It's both engaging and eye-opening."
(*People's World*)

The Slackers
"Gordon's faith and perspicacity in translating Cunhal/Tiago's sizable *obra* into an eight-volume set of tales of war, peace, political struggle and prison in plainspoken, absorbable English is a godsend for armchair travelers—and great reading."
(*People's World*)

Foreword

By Eric A. Gordon

THE Spanish Civil War (1936-1939) represented the defining social issue of its time. With fascist régimes already established in Germany, Italy and Portugal, alongside militarist authoritarian states such as Japan, many millions around the world perceived the fascist danger in Spain and responded to the call. They knew that a fascist Spain, supported by the other fascist nations, would pose a threat to Western democracy in the rest of Europe. Such an axis of forces could only be a threat as well to the young socialist Soviet Union. A fascist victory in Spain would embolden the world's anti-democratic reactionary entente among Junkers, capitalists, colonial imperialists, feudal latifundists and the Church.

Once the war broke out, volunteers streamed in from many lands, representing various political tendencies—Communist, Trotskyist, Socialist, anarchist, syndicalist, Republican— reflecting the different strands of domestic politics within Spain itself. From the United States at least a couple of thousand passionate young men and women joined with those from other lands in the reverently remembered International Brigades. The American contingent was called the Abraham Lincoln Brigade. To this day the Abraham Lincoln Brigade Archives (ALBA) continues to educate the world about these heroes, the last of them deceased now, who risked and gave their lives in the defense of democracy. Their well-researched periodical *The Volunteer* is replete with their stories. When, following World War II, the volunteers came under investigation for their pro-democratic views by such bodies as the House Committee on Un-American Activities, they were dubbed "premature anti-fascists" for presciently recognizing the threat that would soon engulf the whole world.

It's highly ironic to recall, at this writing in 2021, that somehow "antifa"—anti-fascists—are now considered contemptible in conservative and right-wing circles, when millions of Americans, not to mention many more worldwide, were fearlessly, fiercely committed to the "antifa" cause in the 1940s, and won. Perhaps this helps to clarify which side people in those circles are actually on!

As the preeminent place in the world where fascism could be stopped in its tracks, Spain captured the imagination of artists around the globe—poets, novelists, journalists and rapporteurs, photographers, filmmakers, graphic artists, choreographers, singers and songwriters.

Well-known novels by Ernest Hemingway, Alvah Bessie and other Americans captured the sights and smells and passions of war, while British writer George Orwell's *Homage to Catalonia* documented how the defenders of democracy actually went about building the new society within the shell of the old—and under shellfire from the unrelenting fascists. Documentary films such as *The Spanish Earth* powerfully brought the struggle of the Popular Front to viewers.

In other countries, too, of course, artists tried to sound the alarm against fascism. The bold graphic arts of the period attest to widespread appeals for funding for ambulances, arms, refugee relief and other war-related causes. Spanish artist Pablo Picasso's mural-painting *Guernica* may be the single most identifiable artistic response to fascist terror, and is certainly one of the signature art works of the 20th century. To be sure, there also exists a library of pro-Franco apologetica in various media.

Paul Preston, emeritus professor at the London School of Economics, has estimated that books about various aspects of the Spanish Civil War "number somewhere in the region of thirty thousand."[1]

In all of this artistic and historical output, mention is scarcely found of the response to the Spanish Civil War from neighboring Portugal. This is strange since Portugal had already been suffering under António Salazar's fascist regime for almost a

---

1   Paul Preston, "Never More Alive: Kate Mangan's Spanish Memoir," *The Volunteer*, March 2021.

decade and was all too familiar with what lay ahead for the Spanish people—and the world—should the forces of Generalísimo Francisco Franco win. It's our hope that the release of this novel in English will help to fill some of that gap.

Álvaro Cunhal (who would later write his works of fiction under the name Manuel Tiago) was a leader of the Portuguese Communist Party. In the early 1930s he was a leader, and as of 1935 the secretary general, of the Federation of Portuguese Communist Youth. In July of the following year, when he was almost 23 years old, he was sent to Spain on a special mission, to free from a prison in Cáceres two Portuguese comrades, Manuel Guedes and Pires Jorge. He would also assist in getting comrade Francisco Paula de Oliveira home from Moscow.

In Cunhal's own words (my translation), "A few days after I arrived in Spain, Franco unleashed the fascist coup, and the border with Portugal was occupied by the fascists a few days after that. Meanwhile, I had occasion to contact the Communist International, and transmit to them the Party's decision that Francisco Paula de Oliveira return to Portugal. With the border under fascist control, I went to France via Catalonia; Francisco Paula de Oliveira joined me in Paris and together we planned our clandestine maritime voyage, arriving in Lisbon at the beginning of 1937."[2]

In *A casa de Eulália*, the reader will immediately be struck how closely the character of António conforms to the author's own experience. Unquestionably, he was wrestling in his later years with the memory of events he had lived through personally, trying to consolidate their lasting meaning in fictionalized form. It becomes ever more evident why he might have chosen to write under a pseudonym, as similar seepage of autobiographical data into his fiction occurs in many other works. At the same time, the fictional format allowed him to also incorporate incidents and representative persons he either knew himself or whose histories he had learned.

---

2   From Álvaro Cunhal, *Duas Intervenções numa Reunião de Quadros* (Two Speeches at a Meeting of Cadres), Lisbon: Edições Avante!, 1996, 113-114. It bears mentioning that similar adventures in evading frontiers are recounted in Manuel Tiago's books *Five Days, Five Nights* and *Border Crossings* (both International Publishers).

While this novel is written from a Communist point of view, other tendencies active in the defense of the Spanish Republic—or the Spanish Revolution, as some saw it—are present. Yet the writer assiduously avoids polemics that might threaten to divert the narrative away from the main characters and their awesome wartime predicaments. If anything, he underplays the contributions toward the Republican cause made by the Soviet Union, and by Communist volunteers from all over the world, preferring to lift up, at one point, a shipment of rifles from anti-fascist Mexico. For the most part he leaves the factional ideological rivalries simmering off on the sidelines.

In my own judgment, Tiago is at his best form as a writer here developing his rounded characters out of their specific actions. One notable feature is his portrayal of several women, both on the military front and on the home front, in many cases fully as brave and heroic as the men beside them. The liberation of women from traditional patriarchy was, after all, a major goal of the Popular Front against fascism. Aside from the leading characters, Tiago also places the reader amongst the Spanish masses, uprooted, suffering, oppressed and terrorized by war. Their collective portrait is as poignant as anything that happens to the principal figures in the novel.

The use of language in this novel may not be entirely unique in the history of literature, but it is notable. The Spanish and Portuguese languages are very close in vocabulary and grammar, though there are some surprises and unique features. Spanish has pure vowels (and diphthongs such as *ay*, *oy*, *ia*, *io*, *ue*), and most Portuguese speakers find it relatively straightforward to understand Spanish speech. Portuguese, however, also has several nasal vowels (like French) and unpronounced or barely pronounced schwa-like vowels, and many more consonantal sounds, such as *zh*, *sh*, and *z*—not to mention a *b* quite distinct from a *v*—which once existed but have effectively disappeared from modern standard Spanish. And Portuguese has a hard *d* and soft and hard *g*'s, similar to French, not the fricative sounds of Spanish. Perhaps this is not of essential interest to many readers, but the point is it's harder for Spanish speakers to understand Portuguese.

The novel takes place in Spain. What Tiago uses extensively is the Portuguese speakers' partial assimilation and accommodation to *español* after they have resided in Spain for some time. They are so used to speaking in this kind of "Portuñol" that unconsciously and naturally they even use it with one another. Tiago saw no need to "translate" this mash-up of the two languages for his readers, as he would quite reasonably expect them to understand every word of it.

What should a translator do? Try to replicate this nonstandard linguistic evolution into English? As a general rule, I've decided not to. "Portuñol" it may look like to the Portuguese reader, but that charming, almost pidgin language became for these characters the dominant idiom they spoke for ready communication, and that's what I feel is the translator's job to render.

What to do about accent marks? António has an accent in Portuguese, but in Spanish does not. Same with the eponymous Eulália (in Portuguese, but not in Spanish). So with names I've opted to keep the correct accents in their native languages for both the Portuguese and the Spanish characters: The Portuguese António will keep his accent, and the Spanish Eulalia will lose hers.

Once again I have the pleasure of expressing my gratitude to those dear friends and colleagues who read the manuscript of this book and offered their honest, helpful suggestions: Bill Gregory, Francisco Melo, Gary Bono, Janice Rothstein, John Mueter, and Rich Eisbrouch.

I reserve a special place in my constellation for José Oliveira in Portugal, who has reviewed every one of the Tiago books not so much for the fluency of the English but for the accuracy of the translation. How he acquired his fine command of English I have never learned, and perhaps it doesn't matter. We have only communicated by internet, never spoken a word to one another, but I recognize in José a fellow lover of words, of precision of expression, of the power of literary communication, and of history. I do not consider myself a fluent speaker of Portuguese (and the Portuguese I studied was Brazilian), so there are some nuances he suggests that he feels are closer to Tiago's meaning than what I had originally captured, and some idiomatic expressions that defy logic and escaped me on a first reading. I applaud his thoroughness and bottomless, humble goodwill in helping us complete what has become an extraordinary project of bringing all of Álvaro Cunhal's fictional work to the English-reading public.

About the illustrations

THE illustrations we are including in *Eulalia's House* come from a spiral-bound portfolio of *Estampas de la Revolución Española 19 Julio de 1936* (Prints of the Spanish Revolution, July 19, 1936). They are chosen from the 31 full-color watercolor paintings included in the publication. The artist signs his name Sim XXXVI but is otherwise unidentified except in the brief introduction as "a son of the people." It has since been established that the artist was José Luis Rey Vila (1900-1983), who left Spain in 1937, settled in Paris and never returned to his homeland. He used a pseudonym to protect his family.

This portfolio was published in 1936 to raise funds for the *Confederación Nacional del Trabajo* (CNT) and the *Federación Anarquista Ibérica* (FAI), the National Federation of Workers and the Iberian Anarchist Federation. The very fact that the album speaks of the "Spanish Revolution," instead of what may be more familiar formulations such as the "Spanish Civil War," "defense of democracy," or "defending the Spanish Republic" or "stopping fascism," may have already alerted the reader that politically speaking these illustrations come from a distinct sectarian orientation.

I remember so clearly the day and place I purchased this volume, which has remained in my possession ever since. It was at the Communist Party building on West 23rd St. in New York City, where I was living in the 1980s. The building used to have a library, and a bookstore on the street level, and from time to time they held sales of used books they had no space for or desire to retain in their collection. No doubt for reasons of political difference, this book was on the sale table, in close to mint condition. I recall that I paid $2 for it.

"When art becomes the interpreter of some great national sentiment, it is sublime," the introduction reads. "It is as though some great singer of the sagas were relating the heroic deeds of his people, a mingling of the flesh with the spirit. And this is what is represented here. This album is the artistic essence of a great and pure movement of the masses. A movement towards emancipation of a kind that is worthy of the race, in which heroism is unfolded, and here [is] displayed the generosity of those ideals with which a people [is] moved."

And that is the spirit in which we choose to recall to the world these mostly forgotten artistic expressions of the Spanish Civil War, which so powerfully capture the energy and movement, the elation and the despair that Manuel Tiago describes in his novel. The reader will soon see that when spontaneous militia formations emerged, little attention was paid to political orientation. Communists, Republicans, socialists, trade unionists, syndicalists and anarchists all fought side by side in the historic battles of the early months of the war. It was a true popular front of the people, though the cracks in it were certainly apparent.

Not to say that Tiago is oblivious to these divergent strands. At more than one point in this novel he is explicitly critical of the anarchists, though he also admires their courage, heroism and positive contributions. And who can say that any party in those most trying times acted nobly and correctly 100% of the time? Historians still question and debate the fact that though the Soviet Union was among the very few nations in the world that sent substantive assistance to the Republican side, it ended its support in 1938, and with that, the famous International Brigades that came from many lands to defend Spanish democracy were sent home. Many of their bodies, of course, had fallen in Spain and are still there as an eternal testament, even if their graves remain unmarked and unknown.

Let no reader or critic say the publisher is "appropriating" these images as its own. To the contrary. The source is clearly and honorably identified. These paintings from almost 80 years ago are reprinted here (alas in only black and white) in solidarity as a vote for more and greater unity of action in defeating the fascists of our own day.

Eulalia's House

Chapter I

1

SEATED at an outdoor café in the old city, the three comrades conversed and sipped their cool draft beers, whose flavor seemed heightened by the intense heat in the air. Their drinks were the same, but their manners distinct. António was attentive, looking from one side to the other as if expecting something sudden to occur. Manuel watched all around, pleasurably following the girls walking by. Renato, with his leg lazily stretched out, seemed absentminded, barely joining the conversation with just the odd word or two.

To a casual observer brought there from afar with his eyes blindfolded then abruptly uncovered, the circulation on the street, the sidewalks full, people moving about, groups standing in the buildings' shadow—all would seem normal for a Sunday like any other Sunday in summer there in the center of the city, not far from the Puerta del Sol.

So it looked in that corner, in that moment, at first glance. But with prolonged observation, new and strange things could be seen. It was new and unusual that cars would pass by from time to time, interrupting the restful quietude with horn blasts and shouting. It was strange that many men and women prominently wore caps of various styles with letters and insignias. Stranger yet, hearing from nearby streets cracks like the bombs at the Santo Antonio festival, they listened more closely and held still.

At just the moment when António was commenting on the tranquility of their locale, one of those cracks rang out, and the young man, casting a glance toward the end of the street, saw people quickly converging in one place and standing in a group. He said, "It could be, they have killed another person."

Like other émigrés, he spoke in a mishmash of half Spanish, half Portuguese. They had acquired the habit as the most practical for Portuguese people: Everyone would understand them.

"Maybe," Renato said without expression, taking another swallow of his beer.

Maybe, but not certain yet. In recent weeks there had been an increase in attacks on militants and newspaper hawkers on the left. Some had been killed.

On that street, in that moment in the old city, everything was more or less tranquil. But Madrid was a boiling volcano.

Demonstrations and confrontations took place every day. Cars drove by at crazy speeds, their occupants shouting slogans, unfurling their party flags which waved freely in the air. Here and there gunfire broke out, yet curiously, rarely did people chase after anyone.

Rumors spread of a military coup in preparation against the government of the Republic. It was said that the fascists had revolted at the Cuartel de la Montaña, and had closed off the garrison gates to outside contact.

To a nearby Spaniard at the next table, the situation was clear. "If the coup takes place, they are gonna get fucked."

All right, that was one prediction. So for them, the three Portuguese political émigrés sitting there, what would they do in case of a coup?

António worked mornings in a car repair shop. Directly tied to the Party, he performed a very particular task. Knowledgeable as he was about the frontier, usually he was tasked with receiving underground comrades from the Portuguese side and talking them to Madrid, and organizing return trips across the border from Spain to Portugal.

In recent weeks he had been in regular contact with a prominent comrade whom he had picked up at the border. He had come with a special mission which António only partially knew: to secure the freedom of two other comrades who, on crossing the border at the Guadiana River, had been seized by the Guardia Civil, brought to trial for transporting arms, sentenced and imprisoned in Huelva. The comrade never told him his name, and he didn't ask. To António he would remain simply The Comrade, and that's how he referred to him.

Manuel did not yet have a settled life. He had arrived only recently, following a dangerous incident with the youth movement. He hadn't thought about what to do in case of a fascist coup, but he had a general feeling: "I don't know for sure, but I won't be standing around with my arms folded."

Renato assumed a divergent position. He had taken part in the famous workers' strike in Marinha Grande on January 18, 1934. As he was well known in the area, he hid out in the Leiria pine forest. With his wife, he managed to leave Portugal somehow and now they were working—she as a domestic, and he as a shop employee, though it had closed a few days earlier.

"If they have a coup, that's their business. I came from Portugal to stay out of trouble; I didn't come to Spain to get mixed up in more here."

Since António retorted that such a position didn't sound like him, Renato added, "Yes, it does. If I want to make trouble, there's plenty to do in Portugal."

And so they talked that afternoon. It was already twilight before they said goodbye. Renato went to Las Ventas at one end of the city. António and Manuel both went to Puerta del Ángel at the other end, as they were both lodged at the same house.

2

That was Eulalia's house, as they called it.

It was her mother who opened the door to them after spying through a peephole to verify who it was.

It was a period of hatred, assault and revenge. The danger came not from people in the neighborhood disliking Eulalia. To the contrary, it came precisely from the fact that she was respected by everyone and admired by many.

"Madrecita"—Little Mother—as António called her, led them through the corridor to the dining room.

"She hasn't arrived yet," she explained. "She's been out all day. She doesn't eat, doesn't sleep, doesn't rest."

From what people said, the generals all over Spain were involved in the anticipated coup and controlled their units. The Communist Party of Spain—the PCE—was mobilizing its members and launching appeals to the people. Eulalia had no rest.

"She's killing herself, poor thing," Madrecita sighed, but it was obvious that the more she lamented her daughter, the more pride she felt in her.

She treated her guests as though they were family. She called António "Antón," and Manuel "Manolo." She spoiled them with garbanzo and sausage soup with a dash of fresh oil, with lentils, kidney beans, and her most favorite specialty, her real *tortillas*, the omelets she made with eggs, potatoes, a little spicy onion, garlic and parsley. Her art was not only in the ingredients and their proportions—it was in the making. When it was fried on one side, with one quick jerk of the frying pan Madrecita lifted the tortilla off the pan, turned it midair and skillfully retrieved it in flight into the pan, finishing it off frying the other side. Madrecita was pleased with the praise she received for its flavor, and satisfied above all by showing off her talent.

One day António wanted to do it too. Ready for action, he grabbed the frying pan handle. When an intense smell signaled that the omelet was starting to brown on the bottom, he heard Madrecita shouting, "Now! Now!"

He acted. He gave a rapid shake to free the tortilla from the pan, and with one more movement the tortilla flew out from the frying pan like a meteor that he was unable to recapture in space. To the despair of the amateur chef, everyone witnessed the tortilla careening through the air to fall flat on the floor, scattering egg and potato everywhere.

Madrecita didn't get mad. Suppressing the laughter the scene produced, with the figure of her shocked friend standing there, she cleaned the floor and with only the slightest ironic tone, tried to console the poor maladroit. "Don't cry, *hijo mío*, my son. The next time will be better."

That's how they lived in that house—in friendship and happiness.

3

It was António who, through the International Red Aid, had brought Manuel there.

Manuel had clandestinely crossed the border. He tramped though the deserted, silent fields of Alentejo, perilously leaving clues behind him in the howling of dogs that neatly delineated the course he followed in the night. In Rosal de la Frontera he was introduced to António, who brought him to Madrid. Until they reached Seville under a torrid sun, inside the suffocating bus. From there on they took a train, the third-class wooden benches torturing their backs with the disjointed rocking of the old carriage.

António brought him up to date. Things were muddy. The reactionaries did not acknowledge the proclamation of the Republic and a victory of the Popular Front in the February elections with its crushing Republican and Socialist majority in Parliament. "No, they absolutely won't agree to it. They want to retake power by violence. You'll soon see with your own eyes."

The trip passed slowly. António spoke not only of the situation and his assignments. He also spoke about himself—how he enjoyed many other things. That he worked in a car shop as a mechanic. That he had a motorcycle, now busted and waiting to be repaired. "Do you like riding a motorcycle, *amigo*? It's fantastic, my friend!"

Manuel spoke little during the trip. And now, in Madrid, after all that had happened and the dangers that led his comrades to send him to Spain, he felt relieved and of good cheer. For the swiftness of the help he got. For the hospitality from friends in Vale de Vargo. For the calm, well-planned border crossing. For the instant comradeship and welcome he received in the house where António lived.

When he first arrived at the house, Eulalia wasn't there then either. During the trip António had made many references to her. To the comrade's energy, to her militancy. To her activity—which men respected. To the severity of her judgments not only of the fascists but of the whole government, the Republicans, the Socialists—with the exception of Largo Caballero's people. From the way António spoke about Eulalia, little by little Manuel's imagination constructed a sharp image of her even before he ever met her—a thin, self-controlled woman of serious demeanor, a commanding voice, a confident stride and mannish attire.

Then Eulalia arrived, suddenly, bursting into the house, a grown woman with a developed figure, black hair, quick, communicative gestures, a fresh smile. Beauty and happiness invaded the house.

"*Hola!*" she greeted them. "One more child in the house! Good evening, my dears!" And she kissed one and all.

That's how she was, always like that, even in those agitated, anxious days. Someone said of her: A hundred percent Communist, a hundred percent Spanish, a hundred percent woman.

4

In the following days the situation quickly became more aggravated. The provocations and assaults increased in number. António witnessed one of them. He was walking on the street when he heard two gunshots, quite near. Right across the street on the sidewalk a man lurched and fell. A crowd of people approached him and then took off running down the street after the shooter. António never learned if they caught him or not. And if they had caught him? Would they have had him arrested or, in the tide of violence, might someone have right away struck him down? And if that had occurred, who could condemn such an act when fascists were taking aim and murdering by the hour?

"I hate them," Eulalia would say. "Even if he died a thousand times, a fascist would never be able to pay for the crimes he committed."

And she, would she kill someone?

"And why not?" she answered.

Who wouldn't understand her? Not even a year had passed since they assassinated her companion, a militant like herself. Treacherously, right here, at the front door of the house. Riddled with bullets, his face defied recognition.

It's not that the idea of vengeance drove her. It's just that the crime and the pain that touched her directly had given her an almost furious energy to continue the struggle. It's what the situation demanded.

At twilight, on the Paseo de Rosales and at the Casa de Campo, the people of Madrid strolled in search of a little relief from the day's scalding sun. They walked in groups of family or friends. The tragic times the city was living through didn't stop the girls from adorning their hair with a flower or a bow, nor the children from running ahead of their parents laughing and playing. Meanwhile, eyes turned anxiously up toward the now sinister Cuartel de la Montaña. And at the slightest suspect noise coming from afar, people stopped to listen.

The disquiet had its reasons: There was talk of groups of armed Falangists having gone to reinforce the rebellious officers at the Cuartel, and of General Fanjul going there to assume command of the uprising.

Aside from the stories and rumors that circulated, the people had direct cause to fear the worst. One evening, right on the Paseo de Rosales, a car came speeding down that beautiful avenue, firing continuously, mowing people down, and it escaped leaving a trail of fallen bodies, wailing, shouting and blood.

The cruelty of fascist terror showed what would happen if the coup advanced. It was being predicted and was plainly in preparation.

The crime on the Paseo de Rosales confirmed the reason for the apprehension. So António thought, and so did everyone. Only Stockler, that same night, had a different reaction.

This Stockler—a Portuguese—was a strange man, known by that name though no one knew why. Neither did anyone know whence he had come to Madrid, nor what he did before, nor what he was doing now. Some said he was an officer forced to emigrate. Others said he had fled from Belgium where, as a consul, he had facilitated passports for members of the underground. Still others claimed he was an adventurer who roamed all over the world. All hearsay, of course. He personally gave no information about himself other than his opinions. He had come to Spain some months earlier, had hailed the Popular Front victory and supported the Republican government.

Short in stature, his face freshly shaved, with vaguely Indian features, he seemed to be delivering a discourse whenever he spoke. He treated António and Renato with transparent paternalism. He spoke with them, but in what he said, by his tone of voice, by the way he leaned his body, he manifested uncontrolled disdain, as though he were doing them a favor by paying them any attention.

When he heard what had happened on the Paseo de Rosales, he didn't agree that it confirmed the danger of a coup. No, he did not think so at all.

"These are acts of desperation. They don't have the forces. Nothing is going to happen."

He spoke with mannered assurance. It's hard to say if he was fooling himself or if he just wanted to be contrary.

5

To Stockler, António and his friends were people of little education and an off-putting way of life. One event that he witnessed was enough to form his judgment.

It happened on a narrow street behind the enormous building of the Socorro, the Red Aid. One day, passing by there, he was surprised by the infernal, earthshaking noise of a motorcycle. The sound of its growing acceleration was earsplitting. A congregation of young people on the sidewalk watched with curiosity and amusement. With his bike stopped and his feet on the ground, the motorcyclist revved up his engine furiously, preparing his blastoff. The noise got faster and faster and more and more raucous, and suddenly the bike took two jumps forward with one wheel, then the other off the ground, then shot off down the street like a cyclone. And there the biker was with his hands gripped to the handlebars, lifting himself off his seat in a stunt like a gamboling goat with his legs in the air.

"This guy is crazy! He's going to crash!" Stockler mumbled.

The guy didn't crash. He calmly stopped at the end of the street.

Stockler approached him. He was dying to see the face of this madman. Once he saw him, he could hardly believe his eyes. It was António.

António saw him and asked, "So? What do you say, Señor Engineer?" He didn't know why it came out that way, but he called him an engineer.

"You're mistaken, my friend," Stockler answered. "I'm not an engineer." With that he walked away, coldly and without comment on what he had just seen.

This incident was in itself certainly not sufficient reason to prejudice his relationship to António and his friends. But on balance, it carried some weight in how he regarded them.

The people he truly enjoyed meeting and conversing with were of another type entirely, with a different set of acquaintances. As a result, he would stop a moment at the esplanade of the modest bar on a street in the old city where he would exchange a few words with António or Renato, and soon went to another terrace near the Post Office—another sidewalk bar, a different location and different crowd. It was a more select clientele, with some bigshots who now occupied their time in less public activity.

On this other esplanade Stockler sought out the so-called "Hotel Berne Group," three well-known democrats who had emigrated to Spain after the Lisbon police raided the hotel with that name. There a preparatory meeting was taking place for what came to be known, in the police record, as the Delta Plan, a plot for a coup to restore the former bourgeois democratic republic—only the second republic, after France, established in Europe.

They always appeared together. They constituted a true political group, known well enough so that when you spoke of one, inevitably you had to speak of the others. Gossipers called them "the place setting," and liked to speculate which of them was the knife, which the fork, and which the spoon. The joke could have been more or less good-spirited, but the fact of the group was beyond question.

Captain Roseiro could be alternately reserved or aggressive. If in a heated argument he saw he was against the wall with no arguments left, he was capable of interrupting the conversation with a rather unfriendly blast of words and gestures.

One time when he was involved with Stockler in a discussion about the potential for a successful military coup in Portugal, he got tired of arguing and cut off the conversation, saying, "My dear man, I know what I'm talking about. If you don't have the discernment to understand how things are, it's better to shut your trap."

Stockler walked off in a huff. But what had been said was said, and everyone knew how the Captain behaved. By the next time they met, the incident had been forgotten.

Dr. Melxior, talkative and ebullient, liked good food—with the proper drink, naturally. Whenever the conversation was going on too long for his patience, he tried to deflect the group's attention to more enticing subjects.

On one occasion the Captain was severely criticizing the unions at that time for taking over the cafés and bars, and in the end the better restaurants were forced to close.

The Doctor agreed with the union drive, but then surreptitiously added that though they were closed, by chance he knew of one that remained open for its friends. "And, gentlemen, the paella they make is outstanding." From there to the suggestion that they go there for dinner, the distance was short.

The third member of the group was generally referred to only by his name, Fernando Torres, nothing more. It's hard to define him in a few words. He was a mathematician and a renowned, esteemed professor. If you didn't know him as a member of the Hotel Berne Group, it would be difficult to imagine him mixed up in such dangerous activities. But he was indeed involved, yet at the same time he possessed a calm and assured demeanor.

António met with the Group and exchanged impressions with them. They were all agreed on the necessity for

Portuguese antifascist unity. Among the three, it was with Fernando Torres that António established an easygoing, relaxed relationship.

Fernando invited him to his house, where he and his wife welcomed him with warm hospitality.

Talking with Manuel later, António remarked, "He doesn't seem like an intellectual. He's plain and direct."

"What do you mean?" Manuel disagreed. "An intellectual can be plain and direct like a worker."

"It's not easy," António persisted.

"When you speak of him, you are seeing and saying that they exist, *amigo*."

With respect to the three in the Hotel Berne Group, there were different opinions.

"Talk, talk, talk," Renato said. "But doing? They don't do anything."

António disagreed. "The restoration idea won't go anywhere, that's for sure. But they were preparing a coup against Salazar and took a lot of risks, right?"

"All right," Renato conceded, hardly persuaded.

"They've taken risks," António repeated. "And they're thinking about another attempt. Besides, you see them here in Madrid on the Republican side, and you don't see them running scared. They're our allies, and we have to work with them."

"Yes, I guess so," Renato said, closing the conversation.

6

People who came to Madrid in those days from France and Italy couldn't believe what they were seeing. They landed smack in the midst of a big city under a roasting sun, involved in a stormy whirlwind of clashes, demonstrations, armed conflicts and attacks. And contrasts. And surprises. Over here, on a peaceful street, esplanades and people sauntering about. And over there, not far away, caravans of cars with enormous banners unfurled and fluttering in the air. And slogans. And groups of people hurrying to some definite, but unknown destination. And here and there, at any given moment, gunshots, though no one knew where or why.

Among the causes for surprise, Assault Guards, uniformed and armed, joined the demonstrations with the flags of the different parties and, like the popular forces, demanded from the Republican government the immediate distribution of arms.

It was indeed a curious situation. Originally created to defend public order, and conceived in military terms as a specialized force to repress the people in the streets, the Assault Guard at this time turned into a relatively diffuse body whose men were integrated into the defense of liberty and democracy, and of the Popular Front that had triumphed in the elections. Day by day, the fascist conspiracy showed it had occupied dominant positions in the Army. The abuses, the acts of violence, the assaults, the gunfire, the destabilization, were all inspired by fascist groups in a dynamic that contributed to the growing military coup. It was the people themselves who directly defended democratic public order, and alongside them the Assault Guards confronted the provocations, trying to grab and detain the instigators.

During one period, the fascists directed their acts of violence against members and meeting places of the leftwing parties, in particular against the Communists and those who sold *Workers World* on the street. Then they started taking aim at the Assault Guards, at first with isolated acts, until one day when the fascists struck hard and shot a Guard commander dead in an ambush.

That act was practically a pronouncement of the certainty of the coming coup. It could no longer be prevented.

António, Manuel and Renato together attended the funeral. A sea of people filled the vast Post Office Plaza. For hundreds of meters long down the wide avenues, cordons of people holding hands tried to contain the torrent of men, women and youth who ran with their banners shouting slogans. They looked like they were going off to battle more than to a funeral—or better, with the consciousness that this funeral was itself also a battle. Among the slogans, one rose above the others, an urgent demand to the government: "Arms to the people!" From what was known about the stationing of the armed forces, and about the rebellion at the Cuartel de la

Montaña, people were becoming ever more aware that if arms were not distributed, if the people were not armed, the Republic was lost.

The morning after the funeral another piece of news quickly traveled from mouth to mouth. In retaliation for the assassination of their commander, the Assault Guards had shot Calvo Sotelo, who had just returned to Spain a few days before from Portugal, where he had conferred with Salazar.

Stockler emphatically restated his earlier opinion. "That guy was the political leader of the coup in preparation. With the leader dead, the coup is dead."

7

The worsening situation was irreversible, so it appeared. Every day came news of more military units in rebellion. It was already inevitable, to the people of Madrid, that from this armed confrontation could only emerge one conqueror—and the other side conquered. A victory for fascism would be a bloodbath, with terror instituted as the order of the State. Democracy would be freedom. The fascists, however, having gone as far as they had already, would pay dearly for their crimes. One or the other. Any other outcome was an illusion.

The people didn't want to believe the news that floated about. Quiroga, president of the Council, either frightened or a collaborationist, was fired, and his successor, Martínez Barrio, so people said, was negotiating a compromise solution with the rebel generals.

"That would be handing ourselves over to the enemy to drown us in blood," Eulalia protested. "We must stop it, and we will stop it!"

Everyone knew about the Cuartel de la Montaña. "And how about the other military units in Madrid," Manuel asked, "have they all rebelled?"

"No, not all," Eulalia confirmed. According to the comrades, regiments of the First and Second Infantry, and of the Artillery of the Pacific, were with the Republic. It didn't rule out that the government, at the same time it was refusing to hand out arms to the people, continued negotiations with the fascists.

"It's the people who will stop it, friends. And if the government doesn't want to, we'll force it to."

The next day there would be a huge demonstration to get the government to commit to fighting the military rebellion decisively and distributing weapons.

Neither António nor Manuel had ever participated in such a tremendous demonstration, nor even imagined that it could be organized or that they would be able to be part of it.

It looked like all of Madrid had converged on the Puerta del Sol and Gobernación, the government seat. A multitude—what other word existed to express it?—flowed as an ocean with flags and banners. Buses jammed with demonstrators moved in pace with the marchers.

"No to the compromise! Down with the traitors!"

Another cry hurled by thousands of voices echoed the length of the streets. "Weapons! Weapons! Weapons!"

The demonstration turned into an immense concentration of humanity entirely filling the center of the capital.

The people's will, determination and decisiveness made a powerful statement. A compromise would mean the defeat of the Republic. In the situation as it stood now, only the armed populace could save it.

Martínez Barrio would be forced to desist from the treacherous road.

"We will stop it," said Eulalia, confidently and categorically. The huge demonstration strengthened her conviction that it would be stopped.

8

One afternoon, from the Cuartel de la Montaña, the rebel fascists who had entrenched themselves there launched a sortie with two military Jeeps. They forced a bus to stop and, under threat of arms, brought it to the garrison amidst cries and protests from the citizens who saw it happen. One guy crossed in front of them, and they aimed their vehicles right at him, leaving him flat on the pavement and bleeding. The men, women and children on the bus were now hostages. The news spread fast.

Without doubt, the military coup wouldn't be long in coming. Preparing itself for the struggle, the Party was fully mobilized, and its members gathered in their neighborhood offices.

Eulalia returned to the house after dark, excited and nervous. "Today, loved ones, I'm going to leave you," she said as soon as she entered. "They're distributing arms at the Artillery of the Pacific. We're going there."

The rest of them should continue as they had been doing. If things got more complicated they could go to the neighborhood offices. Or else to the headquarters of the Central Committee or the Socorro, the Red Aid.

"It's really a shame, because tomorrow we won't have *churros*," she concluded, breaking the gravity of the news with the humor of her reference to breakfast fritters. With a gesture all her own she gave a kiss to Madrecita and to each of the others.

That's how she behaved, with a mixture of maternal tenderness and the coquette. Churros are what she served for breakfast every once in a while as a special treat.

"And you? When will we see you next?" Manuel asked.

"If nothing happens, I'll be here by morning." And without another word, she left, uninhibited, almost running.

What would they do in case the coup was confirmed? Nothing had been prepared. For António the question was whether or not to go to his auto shop in the morning. In any case he should try to contact The Comrade to find out if he needed anything. Concretely, if The Comrade wanted to return to Portugal immediately, António would have to travel to the frontier to ascertain that the border apparatus was prepared for the crossing.

For Manuel, a decision was more problematic. He had only been in Spain two weeks, supported by the Red Aid, and temporarily at Eulalia's house. Nothing had been settled regarding work, housing or assignments. One thing was certain, though. If the coup happened, he would not simply fold his arms.

Saying which, he glanced at António, as if António would expect anything less from him. Then he added, "You have your Smith, and that's always useful. My hands are empty. You don't fight a war with your fists. If they distribute weapons, I'll have to get one."

Madrecita went to bed. The two comrades, in search of some fresh air, placed themselves at a window opened to the night. Before them, the wide space of the street spread out without any facing houses. Farther on, the winding, leafy slope led up to the Cuartel de la Montaña, whose silhouette, softened by the city lights, could be seen in the distance. The sweltering atmosphere of the Castilian night was almost suffocating, without the hint of a breeze. Everything was calm and silent. The street fixtures, providing a fixed, ordered, continuous light, accented the impression of a tranquil situation.

"If we're lucky, nothing will happen," said Manuel.

"I doubt it," António answered. "I'm afraid of this silence."

Chapter II

1

THEY awoke in the half-light of morning to the blast of cannons. *Boom, boom…boom!* One, two, three, unmistakable, deafening, repetitive explosions.

"It's begun!" António shouted, jumping out of bed and dressing quickly.

They ran down the stairs and out to the street. At that instant a machine gun started popping, and right there to their side, on the façade of a building, they saw a line of pock marks where the shrapnel had hit. Coming from all directions, from both near and far, they could hear isolated rifle shots and salvos, and from time to time the intermittent rasp of machine guns. Two cars sped by, honking their horns. Going in the same direction, toward the center, people were running either by themselves or in groups, some of them with rifles. António and Manuel followed the current.

Along the way, some on the street asked where so many people were headed.

"What do you mean, where? To attack the Cuartel de la Montaña, where else?"

As they neared the center, the gunshots intensified, more cars passed by with banners, and more people had their rifles either slung over their chests on a bandolier or in their hands. Near the Puerta del Sol they saw a lorry surrounded by a shouting crowd with their hands reaching out, a jumble of impatient hands ready to join the combat. From the truck bed they were handing out Mausers.

"Do you know how to use it?" they asked. Without waiting for a response, they explained. "Look, like this," and they pulled the cylinder back—*tra, tra*—and then to the front—*tra, tra*—to demonstrate how the bullet entered its chamber. "Did you understand? Once more, *tra, tra* back, *tra tra* front. Take it!" And they handed down the weapons.

António and Manuel stretched their hands out and received rifles and ammunition.

2

They ran where everyone else was running, through the streets of the old city, more and more surrounded by intense gunfire. It wasn't disparate shots anymore, but an atmosphere dominated by an uninterrupted orchestra of cumulative shooting. Nearby discharges and the hiss of bullets from who knows where, the variations of gunshot sounds from pistol, rifle and machine gun, the simultaneous noises, both in the vicinity and deep in the background, from firing zones in many distant areas, the fading away of some and the intensification of others, the rhythmic resonance from cannon blasts even farther away, echoes answering echoes flowing, and flowing back again, through streets and alleys—the grand and terrifying symphony of urban battle.

The enemy appeared little by little, setting up ambush points in a portal or on a corner, cutting off the movement on a cross street, or sheltering under improvised barricades. Up to this point the two Portuguese comrades were following the stream of armed citizens, firing bullets as the others did, without knowing where the battle lines either began or ended, and without discerning anyone in command.

They were finally detained at a street crossing, where for the first time it appeared there was someone in command, or at least providing guidance. Three or four armed civilians told the others to stay close to buildings and doorways, and proceed forward with caution. Just then, with the roar of rifles overtaking the space, the warnings grew stronger. At one corner, lying on the ground behind a crude barricade, civilians aimed fire against an enemy that the newcomers did not see.

Unexpectedly, those at the barricade stopped firing, stood up with their weapons in hand, signaled the newcomers to follow, rounded the corner hugging the building walls and advanced down the street, now unopposed. At another corner the firestorm started up again, and Manuel and António, with the others, fired too. The fascists, certainly with reinforcements, now attacked from the rooftops, sweeping the streets with showers of bullets.

The wounded fell on all sides. Here and there they lay prostrate. The fighters did not stop to help them. They continued with their advance. Others would come later to help the wounded.

3

"Look!" António suddenly shouted to his companion. Turning one more corner, with the redoubling of violent fire, they saw, a couple of hundred meters ahead, the high walls and the black gate of the Cuartel. Outside, armed civilians in the first lines, and soldiers dressed in the uniforms of their units loyal to the Republic, aimed at the top of the walls where the fascists were shooting continuously. How to advance? In front of the wall and the gate was only open ground with no shelter.

The resistance didn't last long. The battle was decided that very morning. Contrary to any expectation on the assailants' part, the gates opened, and pell-mell, in shirt sleeves and waving white rags high in their hands, dozens of soldiers rushed out across the flat field.

Gunfire from behind felled some of them. Then, for a few brief minutes, the firing ceased. At that point, coming from all directions, soldiers and hundreds of civilians, some armed and some not, advanced toward the Cuartel, breaking through the gate and entering inside. Manuel ran fast and went in too. Outside, a furious fusillade could be heard. Besides the shots from rifles, machine guns and pistols, now there were also explosions from grenades.

António did not pass through the gate. A group of the attacking comrades had formed a barrier, not allowing passage to the avalanche that had massed within minutes, to which were now added trucks and cars with more people shouting and waving banners.

"No more people, *compañeros*! The rebels have surrendered. No one else! You can't go in, *compañero*! I can't let you go in."

Later they found out. Those who entered the Cuartel saw a terrifying scene on the parade ground. The hostages kidnapped on the bus—men, women and children—were all lying on the ground, some stretched out, others in contorted positions, slaughtered, spattered with still fresh blood.

A good number of the soldiers had risen up, opened the gates and passed to the Republican side. Others, with their uniforms removed, were allowed to follow them peacefully. The officers surrendered also. The response to the crime was inevitable. When they saw the officers' uniforms, those first in the line of assault shot to kill. Madrid's military garrison, which went rebel under the fascists, was defeated by the people in arms.

"To Carabanchel!" came the shouts from one truck.

"To Carabanchel! To Carabanchel!" others picked up the charge.

It almost seemed like it was all planned, anticipated and organized in advance. In a few minutes, trucks and cars filled with clusters of humans, and the march turned in reverse.

At the very moment António stepped up onto a truck, out of the blue Manuel also jumped up to his side, as though they had never been separated in the attack on the Cuartel. But it wasn't by chance. Manuel had seen him from afar and run to reach him.

"All the better, let's go together!" he said, breathing hard. "Hey, *amigo*! What good luck!"

4

Passing through streets full of people yelling, "Victory! Victory!" the column ended leaving the capital by the Puerta del Ángel.

In the uncovered truck in which the two Portuguese were traveling, they happened to be right next to a gregarious, talkative young man named Juan García—he told them right away—as though he were counting on a lifelong friendship from that moment on.

"Portuguese? Okay, *compañeros*. We're brothers, right?" and he stayed close by them the whole trip to keep them informed.

He told how the fight had gone since early morning in front of the Cuartel. When the people started the siege, the fascists opened the gates and brought a machine gun and cannon out to the street. Two or three times they fired the cannon on the crowd that had begun forming in the distance. Dead and wounded fell. It was then, at the end of the avenue, that one group made the decision. *Dammit, they had balls alright!* Someone took the wheel of a delivery truck. Others took positions alongside him, with another group leaning on the roof of the cabin. The truck pulled out and proceeded in a mad race, meantime the comrades always firing at the fascist machine gun. The truck went faster and faster until it stopped and crashed against the machine gun and cannon in a thunderous cloud of ruins and dust. Nice, huh? The fascists continued to fire while gathering their dead and wounded, went back into the Cuartel and closed the gates after them.

"That's how we are, we Spaniards!" Juan said. "The Cuartel de la Montaña is ours. Now it'll be Carabanchel."

After a minute he added, "You know what's the worst that could happen? We arrive and everything is over. They say there are soldiers loyal to the Republic there."

Carabanchel was a military barracks on the outskirts of the capital housing several regiments. Soldiers from Madrid units loyal to the Republic, and the people in arms, had begun the siege.

"The same's gonna happen like in Madrid," Juan García insisted. "I'm sure, *amigos*, sure of it."

5

The popular forces controlled the encampments from the surrounding mountains. From there they could look down on the lower terrain and the compound of ochre buildings. The sound of intense shooting died away across the many kilometers of broad skies covering the encampments. The people had cut off the roads with heavy rifle fire and descended the slopes, forcing the troops to recede. Under orders from the fascist rebel officers, those troops had left their garrison to go out and take Madrid.

António and Manuel advanced with the others, following commanders who emerged spontaneously from the masses.

At a certain moment they noticed a young boy, almost a child, unarmed, who had joined them and remained close by. Manuel managed to draw nearer to him. "What are you doing here? Go back! Or do you want to die?"

The boy didn't answer. Also trying to shield himself from fire, he continued to follow them.

"Go back, are you crazy?" Manuel stopped so as not to allow him to pass.

Then the boy responded, as if they were conversing not under fire but in a tranquil locale in the city. "If you fall, I'll grab your rifle."

Manuel, who'd been a Communist since he was a kid, didn't insist. "Come then, come," he replied.

Now it was he sheltering the boy and taking care that he not slip away.

The advance was slow and fitful. At one moment the group to which the two had attached themselves encountered greater resistance. Entrenched behind a hidden outcropping of the hillside, the fascists swept the field with machine gun fire.

It was then that António saw Manuel jump out from his improvised cover behind some rocks and run, trying to remove himself quickly from the combat zone, pocked by constant little clouds of earth when the hailstorm of bullets hit. Next to him was the little unarmed Spanish boy. António lost them in the distance, much farther down the hill. The machine gun fire continued, sounding more and more furious by the minute, when suddenly the situation changed. The entrenched fascists had been fired upon from the rear. The machine gunning stopped. António and the others took advantage of the break in the fire and advanced fast. The displaced fascists made a disorderly retreat down the hill, leaving two bodies behind on the field.

Juan García, who had not left the Portuguese men's side since he bonded with them on the truck, advanced side by side with António. Now that the resistance of the machine gun nucleus was crushed, they pressed on, side by side and confident. "What did I tell you?" Juan shouted. "Carabanchel is ours!—"

He was going to say something more. António turned around to respond when he saw him drop—a few feet behind, his body contorted, his face to the ground.

Many groups of the civilians descended from the hills, converging on the garrison. Some found cover, others ran. The response grew weaker and weaker.

On this stage of the advance, among a group running maybe fifty meters away, António thought he glimpsed The Comrade, joining the firefight like the others. It was just a glance, and he didn't see his face. But it really looked like him, by his long, lanky figure, and above all by that yellow shirt, the same color shirt António had seen him in the night before.

It can't be possible, he thought, straining to look once again. The man had melted deeper amongst the others, but that figure was distinctive. *It's him, it's him!* Later, doubt set in. *That would be crazy.* And he didn't think about it again.

The compound was overtaken by assault not much later. In the barracks themselves, officers loyal to the Republic had resisted the uprising. The fascists had slaughtered soldiers who had refused to continue fighting. Others disobeyed orders and turned themselves in, shouting "Long live the Republic!"

After the Cuartel de la Montaña, Carabanchel. Without taking anything away from the military who were loyal to the Republic, it was once again the people who were decisive.

6

At midday, under a high sun, residents of Puerta del Ángel attended the victorious forces' entrance into the capital. It's impossible to imagine such an unusual, fantastic parade.

They came in military vehicles, some of them with cannons hitched behind, in trucks, in all kinds of cars. They streamed in as crowds, many of them embracing, soldiers and civilians who were joined along the way, forming groups, by young women and children. The soldiers appeared as no one had ever seen them—in shirtsleeves or in unbuttoned uniforms to assuage the heat. Some had steel helmets identifying who they were. The civilians brandished their weapons and shouted slogans in chorus that filled the air so much that you could hardly hear the sound of the motors. Along the whole length of the avenue they came in on, and then on the periphery streets, there were so many people, the gathering so dense, that the only question was, Where did such a multitude come from to arrive at exactly that place, the Puerta del Ángel? Cheers, voices, shouts, all fused into one single clamor of joy and victory.

At the entrance to Madrid, not far from the Casa de Campo, as the parade passed, piercing through the general sound of cheering, one demand could be heard that came out of who knows where:

"Helmets down! Helmets down!"

It seemed absurd, in a war that had just started, to throw down such a precious element of self-defense. Why such a demand? And why was it taken up so fast, first by a few voices, then more, then by hundreds of voices? Why, if not to make clear the reality revealed that day in Madrid? At the Cuartel de la Montaña, then at Carabanchel. The armed forces mobilized by the military hierarchy and commanded by generals and the fascist officialdom had been defeated by the people in arms.

"Helmets down! Helmets down!"

The people demanded it. And would be obeyed. One after another the military started throwing their helmets to the street.

The clamor rose a pitch: "*Victoria! Victoria!*"

With the noisy clang of steel against steel, and steel on pavement, helmets started making a mountain on the ground.

Here and there, boys and girls, even children, ran around picking them up and putting them on their heads like a carnival game.

In the midst of the festive, high-spirited mood, one graceful girl could be seen not with a steel helmet but with a Jesuit skullcap.

Someone in the immense mass of humanity laughed. Others didn't find it funny. There was even one voice that could be heard: "The anarchists in action. They've started—"

On the way out of the Casa de Campo, short blasts of bullets could be heard.

7

Returning to Madrid with the victorious cortege, António headed for The Comrade's house. It was António himself who, as directed by the Party and Red Aid, had found housing for him as part of his duties.

The Comrade was already aware of the fascist defeat at Carabanchel. "The comrades told me—" and then he kept quiet.

Wow, António thought, *the news traveled fast*, and said he had been there himself. He felt quite confused. By the incredible speed with which the news had gotten to The Comrade in his house. By the indifferent affect of his tone when he spoke of such a significant event. And then—or was he mistaken?—by the yellow shirt, now quite distressed, that The Comrade was wearing and that António thought he had seen in the Carabanchel attack.

The conversation stopped for a few awkward moments. Then The Comrade spoke again and explained.

Spanish comrades had already come to the house to bring him up to date on the situation. According to what was now known, Moroccan troops brought in by Franco had turned up in the South along with some red-beret Carlist *Requetés* as the main combat forces. They spread terror with extreme ferocity. Overall, the military units had supported the coup. The fascists had advanced to the North through western Andalusia, and advanced to the South through León and Old Castile, going through Salamanca and Valladolid. The danger now was at the sierra of Guadarrama, Madrid's natural defense, and in Talavera da la Reina in the West. Meanwhile, if in the northern interior the coup had been successful, from Madrid to the Mediterranean the people had defeated the fascists and supported the Republican government. Asturias was also with the Republic. In Catalonia, the anarchists had the situation in hand. Two columns of armed civilians were advancing on Aragon.

"And Huelva?" António interrupted, noticing the lack of mention.

There were reasons for the question. Because it was precisely in Huelva where the two comrades had been seized a few weeks before by the Guardia Civil, caught while trying to cross the border clandestinely by the Guadiana River. Here in Madrid, people were trying to get the Spanish comrades to intervene and have the government free them to return to Portugal. António himself would have to see to their passage.

"The news isn't good, my friend," The Comrade answered. "From the news we're getting, Huelva is in fascist hands. Nothing is known about our two comrades."

António said goodbye. It was twilight already. He wanted to return to the house to see how things were there and to get news of the other comrades.

8

He arrived as night fell. The broad space in front of the house was deserted. Bullet holes were visible on the façade, holes in the walls, and broken glass. He anxiously ran up the stairs. Madrecita opened the door and, breathing heavily, told him to come in. "*Hijo mío*, you're the first to arrive."

Neither Eulalia nor Manuel had returned. Did António know anything about them? No, he said, he didn't. She was nervous about Eulalia, although a neighbor had seen her around midday at Party headquarters. And Manolo? What could have happened?

António recounted how he had lost sight of him.

"God help us, he wasn't left there!"

Madrecita offered him something to eat and filled a pottery jug with water.

They went on talking. António described what he had seen and what he had found out. Madrecita had gone out to a nearby street to participate in the popular welcome to the victors of Carabanchel.

"I didn't see you there, I didn't see you—"

"It wouldn't have been easy—" and they both laughed.

"I'm going to lie down for a bit," said António, dead tired and in need of sleep. "We'll see if I go out again tonight—" He left off the rest of what he was about to say and made a sign that she be quiet too. "Listen—"

They didn't speak. The sudden sound of intense gunfire arrived through the night air, coming from the center of the city.

"The fight's not over, *compañera*," António commented, and he left for his room.

Later on, before she went to bed herself, Madrecita went to his room with the idea of waking him up, as he had asked. But she saw him sleeping so soundly that she hesitated. She made one more gesture toward touching him, but shook her head three times, sighed, and decided not to. She turned off the light that he had left on, left the room and closed the door, trying not to make any noise.

That night Madrid celebrated the great victory of the day. Cars with banners raced through the streets. Trucks full of armed fighters left for the fronts. The occasional ambulance or car leaning on their horn sped through with the wounded. Though the military rebellion had been quashed, machine gun fire could still be heard throughout the city. Now from here, now from there, with varying degrees of intensity, but without cease.

Chapter III

1

THE next morning, when he awoke, António instantly jumped out of bed.

"Madrecita, Madrecita, you didn't wake me!"

"Take it easy, son, here's your breakfast all ready," was her only response.

"Madrecita—" he persisted.

She interrupted. "Don't be angry, Antón. You've got lots of time to win the war."

No, he wasn't angry. How could he be? He left and got on his way.

He thought he would go to Socorro—Red Aid—and sought out the shortest route there through the quiet little streets of the old city. On the way he found Renato, seated at a modest bar terrace, his leg stretched out, a beer in hand, as though the evening before nothing had happened. As if at that very moment there weren't, from both near and far, the crackle of gunfire.

Seated at the same table, also in a detached disposition, was Stockler. Seeing António approaching, he started to get up and leave. Recalling what Stockler had said just days earlier, António beat him to it: "Well, my friend. So there was no coup and the coup failed? And now? What do you say now?"

"Things aren't quite that simple," Stockler answered in a bad mood. "We'll talk some other time." And with that he stood up and departed.

"He's one of those people who are never right and always insist they are," said Renato.

"Look!" António exclaimed, observing someone standing on the sidewalk. "This guy's all we need!" It was Barata, with a three-piece suit and a self-assured composure rare for anyone in those days. Barata was a Portuguese who claimed to be a businessman, yet had no relations whatever with any of the émigrés. "Strange," António said under his breath.

"Nothing's strange nowadays," Renato observed. By then Barata had already passed by and disappeared into the crowd.

António got up and invited Renato to accompany him to Socorro. They tried to find the quietest streets, avoiding the zones from which the most intense gunfire was coming. As they walked, it wasn't easy to find a safe route.

Militarily defeated, the fascists in many parts of the city had gone up to the rooftops crossing from one building to another, and from there fired their weapons on anyone passing by. People responded from below, but it was difficult to aim at them and dislodge them. The gunfire let up when the fighters down below, with repeated blasts from their weapons, forced the men on the rooftops to hold their fire. And when anyone wished to cross the street, they demanded, "*Carnet en la mano!* Show your ID pass!"

People raised their arms with their documents in hand and ran as well as they could to the other side to find shelter from the steady rain of bullets.

The two comrades also raised their arms, hands in the air showing the documents they were holding, and crossed the streets. António walked in a hurry, but Renato's stride was almost slow, as though he were certain that the rooftop shooters would hold their fire until he had passed.

António recounted what had happened with himself and Manuel in the assault on Carabanchel, how Manuel had gone ahead precipitously and wasn't seen again. He was visibly concerned that Manuel hadn't returned to Eulalia's house. But the main thing he felt was enthusiasm for the heroism of the Spanish people, and he could hardly contain a certain pride for having participated in the armed struggle.

"Did you kill anyone?" Renato asked.

"Honestly, I really don't know. I aimed the best I knew how, I fired, I used up all my bullets, the enemy had to retreat, they left dead and wounded on the ground. But it was all of us shooting. I can't say for sure if I killed anyone. I can't even say if I hit my target with any of my shots."

As for Renato, he had seen much, but he had only observed. He had not been given a weapon, nor did he try to get one. He walked through the city, hitching up with different groups that got close to the Cuartel de la Montaña, and had crossed streets battered by the scattershot from the rooftops. But he just observed, nothing more.

"And in this heat," António kidded him, "you find a spot to have a nice cold beer or two, right?" and he laughed.

"Right!" Renato laughed too.

"Did your money come in?" António continued the joke.

"You think I paid all day yesterday and today? Not yesterday and not today either! You sit down, you order your beer and you say '*Uachepé*'—UHP. You know that group? Unite Proletarian Brothers? It was like that yesterday everywhere. Of course it'll be the same today."

2

Morning turned from warm to hot. The streets filled with movement. Men, women, youth and children circulated without really knowing where they were going. The sniping continued on and off. The whole time, cars flying their enormous banners passed at high speed, braking suddenly to avoid running over someone. Red, yellow, purple for the Republican Party, red with the symbol PSOE for the Socialist Workers Party of Spain, red with the hammer and sickle for the

Communists, diagonal black and red for the anarchists. The banners were practically the size of the cars themselves, each one wanting to be the biggest.

Despite the civil war that had begun, despite the news coming from regions occupied by the coup, despite the advance of the fascist troops, the well-known violence, atrocities and the ongoing sniping, the atmosphere in the streets was beyond calm and unworried. In Madrid the coup had been defeated. The people of the capital could breathe deeply. Thousands of people strolled the streets with manifest jubilation.

The two friends shared in the happiness and calm, and the character of that morning would remain forever in their memory were it not for what happened, which they were far from being able to foresee.

They were chatting as they walked, seeking out the best route to the Socorro, when with a hellish shriek of the brakes, a car suddenly stopped next to them. Two militiamen with their black and red berets from the FAI, the Federación Anarquista Ibérica, jumped out, blocked their way, and pointed guns at them.

"Hands up!" they shouted. And right away they wanted to drag them to the car.

People gathered. António protested and tried to explain who they were.

"They're Italians, fascists," said the men from FAI to the crowd.

The danger was real. The anarchists had unleashed a manhunt; it was rumored that at the Casa de Campo it had led to summary judgments and executions.

"We're Portuguese, we're with the Republic, we're Communists!" António proclaimed.

"Communist!" the FAI man laughed. "Fascist is what you are."

Eyeing the scene, a car with the Republican Party banner also stopped. António persisted in protesting, but against his friend's wishes, Renato pulled him quickly over to that car and without asking permission, opened the door to enter. "We're Portuguese Communists. Take us to the PCE, the Partido Comunista de España."

In all the excitement, an argument broke out in the crowd between the anarchists and the Republicans. Meanwhile, the two friends hopped into the car, and it lurched off with the pedal to the floorboard.

Along the way, the Spaniards, although they had rescued the two from danger, did not seem entirely convinced. Only when the PCE vouched for them as persons known to them did the Spaniards say by way of farewell, "All right, you guys were lucky. If it wasn't for us, you'd be eating dust by now."

3

Gunfire, summary executions on every side, General Fanjul managed to escape from the Cuartel de la Montaña. The defeated fascists in Madrid continued fighting in smaller, dispersed formations, hopeful that Franco would arrive in the capital soon.

"We can't just go on walking around," António said. "It's best if we got into the game."

"The game? Perfect!" Renato answered. "With our fists?"

This problem could be solved. António would go back to the house and get the rifle he had been issued in the street. Then they'd look for Eulalia and see if she could get hold of another.

That's what happened. Trying to find the best route, they arrived midday at the neighborhood Party office. Amidst all the hubbub of people coming and going, Eulalia hadn't a moment of repose. She spoke with this one and that one, gave instructions, went inside to fetch something, and all this with her happy expression, her svelte figure, frequent laughter and showing her white teeth.

"You here? What's up, *compañero*?" she addressed António. "And Manuel?" she added, like a hen missing one of her chicks.

António told her why he had come, and how he had lost sight of Manuel at the assault on Carabanchel.

"You don't know anything of him?"

No, he knew nothing more, and it was strange that he hadn't shown up at the house. A momentary shadow crossed Eulalia's face. Then she went in the back and came out with a pistol and some bullets that she gave Renato.

"Will this do? Today or tomorrow—" She was going to say more, but someone called for her. She walked quickly through a door at the back of the office without finishing what she intended to say.

Arriving once again in the center of the city, the two comrades integrated themselves into the popular militias with the same natural ease with which small trickles flow into the torrent of a river. On the street they joined up with a group, and it wasn't necessary to explain who they were. The others accepted them as though they had long been with them, and let them know what they were planning.

António decided not to go to the Socorro that day. "There's no urgency. I'll go tomorrow."

All night long, the fascists fired from the rooftops, moving positions often. And the militia, down below, fired back. There were moments of peace, then others of intense shooting. Unsuccessfully, the militia tried pursuing the gunmen by bolting up the building stairs. They chased people on the street, running blindly. Throughout the night, the forces on the street suffered several wounded. No one could tell if anyone up on the roofs had been hit.

Morning light found them huddled in the space under a staircase, amongst a sizable contingent of militiamen.

Renato had used up all his bullets. Remembering the question he had been asked when he returned from Carabanchel, António asked in turn: "And did you kill anyone?"

"Surely not," Renato answered. "Shots from this pistol wouldn't reach up there, and I'm not a good aim anyway."

Waiting for the cafés to open so he could order something, who should stop right in front of them but Stockler! He seemed like another man. In shirtsleeves, with a pistol at his waist, he looked all revved up. Unlike his usual self, his haughtiness toward the two friends was gone.

"It's fantastic!" he exclaimed. "They wanted a coup, and they made a coup. But the war is won, now it's just cleaning up the city—"

"Did you get into all that sniping yourself?" António asked incredulously.

Stockler didn't bother to answer. He only placed his right hand on his belt, securing his pistol holster.

More than his gesture, it's his sleeve cuff that drew attention. Sewn onto the cuff, two brilliant gold stripes were shining.

Customarily reserved, Renato couldn't hold back. "I didn't know you were a lieutenant—"

"I am now," Stockler retorted, as though he considered the observation rather stupid. "In combat, you need authority."

"Ah!" Renato consented.

"Well, I'm off now," said Stockler as he walked away.

Lieutenant? António asked himself curiously.

Finally, he decided he had to go to the Socorro. Renato said he'd go with him, but before that he wanted to stop back at his house, because his wife Isabel must be very anxious about his not coming home the night before. António also would stop back at Eulalia's house. They agreed to meet up again at noon. And with that, they didn't even wait for the cafés to open. No transportation was running, but spending the whole morning walking home and coming back wasn't too much.

"It's extraordinary," António said before they parted. "I just can't get yesterday out of my head. I got up in the morning and lay myself down at night. It was just one day. And now this. It's hard to believe that so much has happened in such little time."

"Yes," Renato agreed.

Surely neither one of them at that moment had any foreknowledge or idea about what the experiences they had just undergone in those few hours meant for Spain, nor for the world, nor even for themselves.

4

Renato appeared at the appointed hour, and the two proceeded to the Socorro. An unusual spectacle awaited them there. Two days earlier, armed militia guards had been posted at the door, watching the comings and goings of similarly armed people or others seeking arms. Now a sizable crowd of onlookers was observing the unloading of two trucks. In one long line people were moving iron beds into the building, crossing the wide atrium and disappearing deep inside. Others carried boxes of various descriptions and a great variety of objects, proceeding in a disorderly, unconnected manner. Aside from the people with weapons, men and women in white smocks walked around for no perceptible reason.

Elbowing his way with Renato, António approached Gonzalo, the functionary at Socorro with whom he generally dealt. Gonzalo seemed lost in the midst of the confusion. António asked if there were any news for him, anything for him to do, how to make a connection.

Quite uncharacteristically, Gonzalo answered with ill temper. "What do you want me to tell you? Don't you see what's happening? And what the hell do I care what you have to do or don't do? Ask your party, go home, go take a hike, go wherever you want, but let us work." Without another word he turned his back and disappeared.

António took offense. *In other words, there's nothing to do, and we've never done anything, right? It's pretty clear what the Portuguese are worth to them!*

He thought of going after Gonzalo, but desisted. Walking back into the atrium, he and Renato sat at the end of a step on a stone staircase.

Surveying that apparently disconnected movement, the human chain that continued to transport iron beds, various boxes and things, the blur of white gowns, he spoke frankly: "They're crazy, that's all."

But no, they were not crazy. In that seeming disorder, something important and urgent was taking shape: a new field hospital. The hospitals in the city no longer had capacity to receive the ever greater numbers of wounded arriving from the fighting in the streets and that had begun coming in from the various fronts where people's militias were halting the advance of the fascist troops.

A Spaniard with a rifle in hand sat down next to the two comrades, likewise to watch the activity. Thin, with a sharp eye, he didn't miss any detail.

At a given moment the line of transporters of the beds, from the doorway at the street up to the top of the stairs, suddenly stopped. In the doorways to the interior of the building people jammed and couldn't get through.

"What will come of all this nobody knows yet," António pronounced in his bad humor.

"Yes, they know, *compañero*," the Spaniard next to them replied, and he was right. "From all this we're going to get the field hospital that we've been needing."

Without doubt it was a difficult task, almost inexplicable in a situation of complete destabilization and crumbling of state functions. Who set up and got these hospitals working? Who suggested them? Who assumed the organization, the planning, the leadership of medical services, the recruitment of nurses and other personnel? It's simply true that just as there emerged popular armed forces to successfully confront the forces of the armed rebel military, there also emerged, certainly by the initiative of responsible parties but with a high degree of spontaneity and pluck coming from the masses, fully functioning field hospitals.

Now not quite so upset, António asked their neighbor if, besides the sniping, he knew of other combat zones in the city.

No, he didn't. He introduced himself as Pepe, saying that he and other comrades would remain there until nightfall and then go to the Gran Vía, where the previous night the fascists had driven cars at high speed machine gunning everyone. That's where they were headed. If the two Portuguese wanted, they could go too.

5

As night fell, no one lit the lights on the Gran Vía. In the dark you could barely make out the enormous outlines of the buildings. From the direction of the Puerta del Sol came the noise of sniping slicing through the air. On the avenue going down from the Plaza de España, you could hear the footsteps of people who were still moving about in the city.

Here and there stood armed groups. Some of them explained what they were there to do and offered some direction. Spontaneous commanders arose, and people accepted them.

The groups placed themselves in ambush at the corners of the cross streets. If the fascists repeated their earlier action, it was necessary to stop them.

Not much time for explanation had passed before two headlights appeared, glaring from the top of the avenue. People ran through the dark to find cover. The car raced pell-mell down the avenue, opening fire from automatic weapons, sweeping the sidewalks and shattering the shop windows.

At the first, second and third cross street corners shots rang out from rifles and pistols, one after another, but the car, continuing to shoot from its machine gun, passed them all by, ending up disappearing in the Plaza de España at the bottom of the avenue. One dead and two wounded were the yield from that sortie.

"Fuckers!" a voice echoed out of the darkness, breaking the silence that followed.

It didn't take long before the scene repeated itself. This time the car was hit—maybe it was the driver, maybe the tires. But it didn't stop. Even though the steering was erratic, the car continued to fire and managed to get away.

"I shit on your mother!" Pepe raged. He and António and Renato, with their group, had sequestered themselves around a corner. "What lousy aim!"

After half an hour, sudden shooting and noisy skidding could be heard. A car emerged from a cross street, made a quick turn onto the avenue and dashed out with dizzying speed, its headlights on high beam glaring into the eyes of anyone in front of it. The group opened fire. The car came closer and closer, and almost passed when suddenly a figure jumped out from the corner to the middle of the crosswalk, the headlights bearing down on him. *He's going to kill himself! He's going to kill himself!* António thought. But then, surely because the driver's instinct kicked in for a quick reaction, the car swerved abruptly, started spinning like a top and with a thunderous crash landed on the other side of the boulevard, the hood wrapped around a lamppost, the horn continuously sounding like an alarm. Some figures jumped out, still firing and trying to escape alongside the buildings. They didn't get far. One after the other, they fell in the gunfire. Patrols came running to surround the car. Piercing the new silence after the crash came a single shot, from a pistol.

In the prevailing confusion, in the dark, António had trouble finding Renato. Seeing the figure throwing himself in front of the car with his arms raised, António thought it looked like him.

Almost angry about the reckless danger his comrade had risked, he asked, "It was you, wasn't it?"

"So?" Renato answered perfectly calmly.

6

A week passed. Little by little the sniping died out. During the day, but less and less, isolated gunshots could be heard. At night there was still dense gunfire around the city, especially in the narrow streets of the center.

By surprise, Manuel appeared at the house. Madrecita was home. Eulalia was too, in a sullen mood, with her black hair and a pistol in its holster at her waist.

António had been out somewhere with Renato, but no one knew anything more of him.

"*Hijo mío*, my son! how happy to see you, dear!" Eulalia ran to embrace him. "Where have you been? We thought you were dead—"

"At Guadarrama," he answered modestly. "And you?"

She did a little of everything. She was still on the neighborhood committee, organizing things, taking the wounded to the new field hospital, helping to pick up the "cold cuts."

It wasn't a joke. That's how they spoke now about the fallen bodies shot to death that appeared around the city. They had to remove them and take them to the cemetery. Eulalia talked about these things as though they were commonplace. The conversation ran its course with a remarkable lack of apprehension.

"And now, where are you going?" she asked.

He was going back to Guadarrama. He was enlisted in the Fifth Regiment of the People's Militias, which had just been created. He had come to the city, but he would return to the front that same day.

António had been very anxious not knowing anything about Manuel since Carabanchel. Shouldn't he have expected Manuel to return to the house?

No. They couldn't wait for each other.

They talked for hours about the situation, about the victory of the people of Madrid and the development of operations to the north, the northeast and southeast of Madrid.

Then the conversation took another turn. Up until then, in those troubled days with nary a spare minute, Eulalia had never asked him what had happened that forced him to emigrate. On this day she posed the question directly. "So really, what happened with you, my dear? So young and already so dangerous!"

It happened in Lisbon during the Public Fair. The whole population was in the streets. The Communist Youth had taken the daring initiative to do some agitational work. Two comrades circulated through the crowds handing out manifestos. He, Manuel, followed them at a certain distance. In case the police should appear and want to arrest the comrades, he would intervene and prevent them from being apprehended. All went well until a plainclothes policeman discovered them and declared them under arrest, pointing a pistol at them. Manuel quickly approached him, pointed his own pistol at the policeman's back and told him to let go of the comrades. The policeman spun around and fired, but Manuel fired first. The two comrades fled into the mass of people shouting, "We're Communists! Long live freedom!" He, Manuel, was about to do the same, when at his side he heard a voice.

"I know you, you devil! You're Rascal's son!"

Rascal was his father's nickname. The man made an attempt to seize him, but the people in the crowd opened a path for him to escape and closed it to prevent the man from following.

That is what actually transpired, but Manuel did not recount it in such detail. He said only that at a propaganda affair, having the task of defending comrades handing out manifestos, he had to open fire, he wounded a policeman and was identified, then the comrades had sent him to Spain for a while.

"What balls!" Eulalia exalted. And she touched his face admiringly—almost motherly, but Manuel felt it as the ambiguous caress of a woman.

7

At the Socorro, António found an urgent message. The Comrade needed to speak with him. António should go see him, and he did.

The lady of the house opened the door and led him directly to the room.

In an atmosphere heavy with smoke, The Comrade rose to greet him. His hair all awry, he had certainly been scratching his head as he wrote. Owing to fatigue, his torso didn't seem steady atop his thin, excessively long legs.

The issue was not complicated. He wanted to return to Portugal as soon as possible. "My job isn't here, it's there," he said in a shaky voice.

He had dealt with what he had to do. Now he wanted to return before things got any more complicated.

António should go to the border and prepare the crossing. How he'd get there he didn't know; he'd have to work with the Spanish comrades. Obviously it would not be easy to decide where to make the crossing. The Portalegre mountains were out of the question, because Cáceres and the surrounding region were in the hands of Franco's troops. The whole area of Vale de Vargo and Rosal de la Frontera was probably also occupied. They could try through Elvas-Badajoz although it had been months since anyone had passed over there. That's what they decided. António was all ready to leave when The Comrade asked him to sit down again.

"There's something I want you to know. I appreciate very much what you have done. You, Manuel and the other comrades. But I think you shouldn't put yourself in the line of fire. You have responsibilities in our party, you have assignments such as the one we've just been discussing, and you shouldn't take such risks."

How should António receive such an opinion? As praise for his responsibility as a representative of the PCP there in

Madrid? No. He received it with displeasure because he felt gratified with his own conduct, and that of Manuel and Renato. In a certain way, he saw The Comrade's words as a criticism. And suddenly there came to mind the suspicion that had stayed with him since the assault on Carabanchel, when he thought he recognized precisely The Comrade with a rifle in his hands, firing and participating in the attack on the garrison. Irritated, he shot back, "And you? Were you there, yes or no?"

"No," The Comrade responded plainly, without hesitation.

"Fine, better then, because your work is in Portugal."

Things would have remained settled in his mind in that way if, in the course of contacting the Spanish comrades, the suspicion had not surged again ever more forcefully. He, António, had been present at the attack on the Cuartel de la Montaña, at Carabanchel and many other sites. He had said so to The Comrade. If he had not mentioned the site when he asked The Comrade if he had been "there," how could he have responded "no," if by their conversation he hadn't believed it was Carabanchel that António was talking about? And if he did understand that António was referring to Carabanchel, he could only have understood it having been there.

I caught you, you rogue, he happily concluded to himself. *We'll see you again sometime and you'll have some explaining to do!*

It wasn't irritation any more. Rather, he seemed to gain awareness that if what he had concluded was true, he did not find the criticism justified, but more than that, he felt satisfaction with himself and with his comrades. *If he acted in that way, then we also have the right to do so.*

8

Yes, the possibility existed of getting to the border. Early the next morning a small column of militia in the recently formed Fifth Regiment was departing for Badajoz. It was critical to grasp the situation. Cáceres to the north and Seville and Huelva to the south had been occupied by the fascists. But Badajoz was still in Republican hands. That was the possibility. He could go in the column if he wanted.

"Clearly I want to. That's why I asked for your help."

A few hours later he was introduced to a comrade in the column, and António was told to discuss everything with him.

Rubio was a young man—blond, like his name, with his blue eyes and facial features to match. His golden hair and the stubble of his unshaven face looked like end-tips of wire. His voice was high-pitched and he talked a lot, accompanying his words with rapid gestures, at times too much.

"We'll go together, brother. I'll introduce you to all the *compañeros*. You'll travel under my protection, and I'll help you in everything you need."

António agreed. Early in the morning they met at the Plaza de España, where the column formed, with two freight trucks and an automobile. All told, they were a couple of dozen armed civilians. António left his rifle at home. He preferred to carry his Smith 32, which had been given to him a few days before. It was more appropriate for the kind of mobility required on this mission. He hadn't had the chance to try it out yet. That would have shown its value.

Rubio pointed to the truck they'd be riding in. Shortly after, the column started on its way and they left Madrid.

In the pale clarity of dawn the still, silent atmosphere enveloped the fields in a dewy sparkle. But in the east the red blush of the sky promised the unbearable heat that was to come.

Chapter IV

1

THE column selected the safest route—well south of Talavera de la Reina, where there had been reports of heavy fascist attacks, and then even farther south of Toledo, where they'd cross the Tajo—the Tagus River. They passed villages and crossed highways. From their vehicles they saluted and, by word and gesture, gave encouragement to everyone they saw along the way. So the day passed, rolling over the Castilian mesa under the burning sun. In the late afternoon, a car facing the opposite direction made a signal for them to stop. It was dangerous to proceed along that highway. Some twenty or thirty kilometers ahead the fascists had taken and occupied positions. Following that advice, the column took a semi-paved secondary road that disappeared in a straight line over the plain.

Their progress under a scorching sun was painful. In the cargo trucks, with no roof, men roasted, swamped in sweat. Not even the movement through the air helped. On the contrary, the very air burned their skin and choked their breath.

The trucks produced clouds of reddish dust that remained suspended midair kilometers long. The road beaten by the sun for hours, a quiver in the air distorted normal vision.

At nightfall the column reached a village that extended alongside the road, with small cottages, doors and windows all alike. Some militiamen right away jumped to the ground to stretch their legs. Some had their weapons across their chests, others left their guns on the truck. Not a soul was in sight. They knocked on some doors, but no one answered. Finally an old couple appeared and explained what had happened.

The previous night, a group of families fleeing from the direction of the border had arrived in the settlement. The fascists had occupied towns and were shooting people one after another. Those who managed to escape ran into the fields to find refuge. The group that had shown up here had come by the road carrying the alarming news. The fascists were not far away.

One of the arrivals stood out for his nervousness and anxiety. He couldn't stop talking and gesticulating, pushing those who had stopped, insisting that they continue to run without delay. "They're killing everyone. Men and women. Not even the children are spared. They'll be here before long. You have to keep marching."

The refugees barely drank some water from a well before they started up again on their journey.

People from the area couldn't sit idle any more. During the night and the following morning, they quickly organized whatever they could and, abandoning the road, got onto footpaths and headed for the fields.

The old couple recounted all this to the column, and questions arose. Why did they, old as they were, stay behind? They explained, slowly and hesitantly. Their son had left on his bicycle to confirm if the fascists were still advancing. "He hasn't come back yet. We're not going without him."

And they offered their house if the militiamen wanted anything. There wasn't much; it was all they had.

"Where are we exactly?" Rubio asked.

"Not far from Don Benito," the old man answered.

"How many kilometers, do you know?"

"Forty or fifty, not more. Still, it's a lot," he added. "They can't advance without the infantry, and the infantry goes on foot. Forty or fifty kilometers is a lot! They won't be here so soon."

Rubio did not agree to such passivity. Ahead of the infantry, motorized units would surely go out on reconnaissance. He insisted it would be best to take measures, but could not persuade the others. Exhausted from the whole day on the road and the suffocating heat, all they wanted was rest. Why the rush? they argued. Maybe the old couple's son on the bicycle would come back with news.

With that general concurrence, they left the road and set up their cars and trucks on a small side street that looked out over the fields. They too drank water from the well, snacked on what they brought with them and settled in to spend the night.

Everyone found their own corner to lie down in, many on the ground next to the houses. António chose to get back up onto the truck. He took his boots off to let his feet air out, and before it got completely dark he was already fast asleep.

2

He jerked awake, only to crouch down into the bed of the truck to defend himself from the hellish gunfire that resounded on all sides. None of his *compañeros* were around.

In the semi-darkness, he saw the tassels on the red képis of the Carlist troops. Firing away, they ran toward the trucks.

All alone, separated from the others, there was nothing he could do but flee, and do so at the first opening without losing any time. He was still searching for his boots that he had taken off before going to sleep. Reassuringly, he touched the Smith he had in its holster. Quickly, without further thought, he jumped from the height of the truck and, trying to ignore the pain in the soles of his feet as he ran across gravel, placed himself between the houses, retreated from the road and, hopping every time something sharp on the terrain cut into his feet, ran through the fields until, out of breath with his feet bleeding, he fell down seeking shelter in a ditch.

The night was serene and hot. It smelled of hay stubble from the grain harvest. Now he heard only occasional gunshots, ever more distant, and the singing of crickets and grasshoppers that populated the plain. Lying on his back, stripped of energy, António looked at the clear, cloudless sky dappled by the random display of sparkling stars. He thought of nothing. Everything was confusion aside from the concrete situation in which he found himself. Later, a flood of disordered ideas and questions occurred to him.

What would have happened to his *compañeros*? Taken by surprise, would they have resisted? Were they dead? Had they fled like him? From time to time he still heard a few gunshots. What was the meaning of each shot? Another comrade discovered and killed? A shot fired on a shadow in the dark? The night calm descended, and the overall silence was now interrupted and dominated by the mysterious, gentle orchestra of insects, attesting that apart from human beings, other living beings are the lords of the land.

Strange though it may seem, he fell asleep again and only awoke to the freshness of dawn's coming, the music of the insects still filling the air. The sky was still splendidly starry. Unlike the violent shock of awakening under fire in the truck, now he awoke clear-headed, with full consciousness of the mess he was in.

He had to distance himself even more from the road, penetrate deeper into the fields, and find some way to get a clear idea of the military situation. How far had the fascists advanced? Where could he find the Republican forces? Where could he find support or refuge? In any case, he had to get up and start walking who knows how many leagues? But then when he stood up, his bare, wounded feet showed him his difficulty. He had no hope of saving himself, wherever that might be, without first resolving that problem.

He made a quick decision. He cleaned his feet as much as possible from the soil and straw that had stuck to his blood. He tore his shirttails and wrapped his feet with strips of cloth as bandages. The acute pains continued, but he had to walk, and this way it would be a little easier.

On the horizon a transparent crescent announced the birth of the new day. The fascists had come from the south and the west. He had to march east, in the direction of the sun rising in territory held by the Republic. Negotiating the terrain as though he were walking on hot coals, he got on his way.

3

The sun was already high in the steaming summer morning when he sat on the ground to rest his feet and look around. To the east and south he could see the plain reaching out as far as the horizon, yellow, peaceful and full of light. No sign could be seen of the cruel war raging over it, the massacres, the destructions, the flight of so many people in search of safety.

To the east and north, now interrupting the horizon line, undulating hills revealed the profiles of trees or green tufts that indicated the proximity of villages or houses. As if to confirm that impression, in the fold of one ripple of land he saw two little cottages ruined and deserted, and from there a sudden slope down through bushes and thickets. Winding down the decline, irregular ochre earthen paths neatly described the natural features and the ancient tread of human feet.

Just a few feet ahead of him, surprisingly, he saw a man standing in the shade of a solitary oak tree. What could a single man be doing in that desert? He stopped. The man looked suspiciously toward António, surely a rare apparition.

"*Buenos días,*" António called.

The man mumbled some incomprehensible words and stiffened as if sensing some combativeness.

"*Buenos días,*" António repeated.

"*Buenos días,*" the man finally answered.

"Isn't there any settlement around here?" António asked.

The man shrugged his shoulders in the face of such foolishness. "What settlement?" And then, almost aggressively, he added, "Where are you going?"

"The fascists aren't far away," António explained.

The man didn't respond. Then he said decisively, "You go your way and I'll go mine." He turned his back, left the shade of the tree and took a couple of steps away.

António also took a couple of steps, hobbling on his painful feet. "I'm missing my boots. I'm barefoot, I can't walk—"

The tone of his words was difficult to pin down—a mixture of imposition and supplication.

"There's nothing I can do about it," the man said condescendingly, and he answered the earlier question. "There's no settlement around here."

António felt dazed by a maelstrom of contradictory notions. There was only one solution. It was a bad one, but the only one, and that was the insistent idea that drove him to make a decision.

"Your boots!" he said threateningly.

"Are you crazy or what?" the man said, raising his voice. "You get on your way, and I'll get on mine."

"Halt right there!" António shouted. "You are going to give me your boots because I have to get to Madrid."

"You're crazy!" the man repeated and made a start to run off.

Then he stopped. Before him he saw an arm extended with a heavy Smith 32 aimed at him.

"Pardon me," António said, "but give me your boots or I will kill you!" The man still hesitated.

"I'm serious, I will kill you!" António shouted, pointing the revolver.

Then, in a quick move, the man sat on the ground, took off his boots and sat there speechless, stupefied, not knowing what to do.

António put the boots on with some difficulty. He nearly howled forcing his wounded feet into them. Fortunately the man had big feet so his boots didn't press on his lesions too badly.

"Forgive me, friend," António said again, keeping his hand on his weapon. "I have no other choice. Forgive me, *amigo*."

He knew any explanation would be absolutely useless and ridiculous. Nevertheless, he felt he needed to at least say that, and much more.

After a few moments he walked away, leaving the other man sitting on the ground, looking stunned at the socks on his feet.

A few steps farther, António stopped and turned around, sad and disheartened, wanting to go back and return the boots to the man. Then he shook his head to shake off any remorse, and he walked off.

4

Hours later, his feet bloody pulps, dying of heat and thirst, famished, he saw an isolated house in a broad, deserted space. He hardly paid attention to the wooden shack, the well with the pulley, the flat yard in front, the carriage with its poles pointing to the sky, the chickens strutting about pecking at the ground. There was cause for greater shock. With the country devastated by war and horrible massacres, the inhabitants were walking around as if life were proceeding normally. A man and a woman were dragging some sacks, and a young woman came out of the house at that moment, completely at ease with her graceful stride.

When the people from the house saw him, they gave no sign of surprise. The man and woman calmly placed the sacks on the ground, and the young woman casually returned into the house. Only when António got to the yard did the couple stop their work and look at him expectantly.

"*Buenas tardes*," he greeted them.

"*Buenas*," the two answered in tandem. They eyed him attentively, without apparent mistrust.

"Do you have a little water to drink?"

"Conchita!" the woman shouted. And when the girl appeared at the door, the woman told her to give some water to the new arrival.

The girl brought a pottery jug. António lifted it into the air, opened his mouth and drank the Andalusian way, allowing the jet of water to stream down his throat. Unskilled at it, though, he gagged a little and his face and chest were left all wet. The girl gave off a hearty laugh.

"Are you going to Campillas?" the man asked quite naturally.

"Yes, I am," António answered, although he didn't recognize that name.

"It's far."

António felt disarmed, not knowing what to respond. At last he spoke up. He had come from afar, crossing the fields since leaving the road to Badajoz. The fascists were advancing and had occupied villages and killed people.

"The fascists?" the man questioned. He did not even know about the military coup. António explained what had happened.

The young woman was standing now in the shade of the doorway, and a young boy joined her, curious to see.

"I didn't know that, but they won't come here," the man commented. "There's nothing here to interest them. Anyway, I'm not looking for any trouble. Why would they do us any harm?"

The woman interrupted her husband in a tender voice. The stranger was poor, he'd come a long way, he must be tired. "Don't you want to eat something?"

How could he refuse? In a few moments they were all inside.

He didn't expect them to invite him to make himself comfortable. He lay back on some sacks that seemed ready to receive him. They smelled of hay and brush, but he couldn't quite identify another specific smell wafting through the air. Potatoes just taken from the earth? Flour? In any event, the smell lent a sense of comfort to the house, shelter and hospitality.

The wife cut a big hunk of bread on the slant—*Where did they go to buy it? Or did they bake it here?*—and offered it to him with a slice of cheese. The young woman started laughing again, seeing him attack the snack with noisy ravenousness.

"Conchita!" her mother chastised. The girl did her best, but watching the stranger furiously devouring the offering, she couldn't control herself and, suppressing her laughter, ran outside with her brother behind.

"Conchita!" the mother repeated. After they exchanged a few words, António lay back again on the sacks, more comfortable now, thinking he would leave. As he considered it, his head nodded, and soon he wasn't hearing what they were saying to him.

The woman took her husband aside, whispered something, and came back. "You can stay here for the night," she said softly.

He couldn't lose time; but he didn't have the energy to get up and resume his march. He started to untie his boots to relieve his feet before sleep.

Calmed down now, the girl reentered the room and sat on a stool to watch him. Suddenly she cried out, "Father, look!"

With his boots off, António's feet, wrapped in strips of cloth from his shirt, appeared beaten, swollen and bloody.

Not knowing why, António felt ashamed of his poor state. He couldn't say how he had stolen the boots, nor could he refuse the help.

They filled a shallow bowl with water for him to soak his feet and got him a cloth to clean them. They observed him in grave silence.

"Here you can sleep in peace. No one will bother you," said the man before he went to bed.

Early the next morning, while the girl and the little one were still sleeping, they gave him bread and a cup of coffee.

He asked once again what they planned to do if the fascists occupied the region and came to the house. They needed to believe him: The fascists would spare no one.

"We're staying. There's nothing they could want here. Why would they cause us any harm?"

5

Everything should have proved Conchita's father right. Truly, what could be of any use to the fascists in that barely inhabited wilderness? Where would they be coming from, and where would they be going? Why and for what would they invade that vast, practically deserted plain?

Before the day ended, however, such optimism was given the lie. Some two hours into his march António encountered three corpses fallen by the side of a path: two men and a woman, dumped willy-nilly, dead, exuding the rotting smell of decomposition. A few hundred meters farther, more bodies, these spread out from one another, as though they had been targeted while escaping. A man, a woman and a child. Earth, blood, flies and ants.

Where had the killers come from? Where were they going? Who were they actually? To what purpose would they assault the desert plain?

"Why would they cause us any harm?" Conchita's father had asked. "There's nothing they could want here."

That same afternoon, that illusion received yet another rebuttal.

Having walked another two or three hours, António came to another isolated house. In front of the door lay a dead man, his face smashed into a red paste in which you could see the open, shocked eyes that death could not close. Across the threshold also lay a dead woman in a sea of dry, coagulated blood, her clothing ripped, skirt raised, her breast bare, and several blows on her chest and neck. Inside there was no one else. The miserable dwelling showed no sign of being ransacked.

Though starving and exhausted, António didn't even remember to search the house for something to satisfy his thirst and hunger. Not even to look for socks for his wounded feet and a shirt to replace the one he'd ripped. The memory of that phrase of Conchita's father kept jumping out at him: "If there's nothing they could want here, why would they do us any harm?"

He sped away as fast as his fatigue and his burdensome feet would permit.

6

Later he peered into the distance and, almost imperceptible but numberless, he saw figures moving like a long train of ants dotting the far-off horizon. Troops? Civilians? He couldn't distinguish closely enough to tell. One indication soon became clear. Whoever it was, the movement was from south to north, which had three possible explanations: Either an advancing fascist column, a retreating Republican column, or civilian refugees.

After another hour of walking it was unmistakable. Along a secondary semi-paved road extended a long cortege of civilians in flight.

Proceeding on foot, in more or less scattered groups, men, mostly older, and hundreds of women, girls and children. Alongside the marchers plodded some mules and burros burdened with a great variety of things. The occasional cart had clusters of children or families mounted atop their cargo. They marched slowly and mutely. The only sounds were the dragging of feet, the animals' stomping on the ground, and the screech of wheels.

António approached and joined the procession. No one appeared surprised. No one asked him anything. No one seemed to notice his puffy, sunburned skin, nor his purplish lips chapped by thirst and the sun's heat. Obviously they had all come from afar, and many, like him, had also joined the line.

At twilight, those at the front chose a campsite on the bank of a puny stream, with a few trees and bushes, where they would spend the night.

Without commotion, they distributed themselves in groups, sitting or lying on the ground. The exhausted children were sedate and quiet. António and others eagerly ran to drink from the stream and wash their faces in its muddy water. Some pulled meagre provisions out of their rucksacks, eating alone or offering something to those nearby.

An enervated António stretched out on his back in the midst of a random group and lay there with his eyes closed. He heard women's voices conversing nearby, but had neither the strength nor the interest to open his eyes and see who they were. He only did so when his ears caught the light sound of a young woman at his side. "Mamá," she asked, "what's wrong with this guy? Is he sick?"

At that point he opened his eyes and saw a girl observing him just at arm's length. Dark-featured, her face wrapped in a kerchief, she had deep black eyes that stared at him curiously. He sat up. No, he wasn't sick, he felt all right. The girl removed herself a few steps and once again sat on the ground. António stretched out once more and closed his eyes.

A few moments later he felt a tap on his shoulder, and that same light voice asked him, "Hey, are you hungry?"

When he opened his eyes, the girl asked no more questions but handed him a piece of bread.

He ate while she, sitting at his feet, stared at him. Now he was fully awake. *Caramba!* He had never seen such a pretty girl!

"What's your name, girl?" he asked.

"Celia," she answered.

Night fell. Everyone adjusted themselves on the ground, some of them nestling together with others. António sensed the girl's nearness and couldn't stop thinking about her dark face with the deep black eyes and the soft, fresh voice. Before long he fell asleep.

7

For two full days he marched with the fugitives.

Generally, people didn't engage in conversation. But when the caravan stopped, he would sometimes talked with one or another, hear their stories. They spoke of recollections, memories, referred to what they had lost. Rarely did they speak of politics. Except for a central idea they didn't even have to express in words because the truth of it stood right there in the tragic procession of a population in flight—the value of freedom, to which people have the right and which they had achieved. It was evident, too, in the horrors and crimes committed against the people—for this desire to live in freedom.

During those two days Celia remained always near António, most of the time by his side, as if they had known one another for a long time. She was attentive, sharing her bread and the available water with him. She sat next to him when they rested. She generously offered her friendship, and it felt like she was seeking it as well.

They spoke little. Only one time, remarking on his pronunciation, she asked him if he wasn't Spanish. No, he wasn't Spanish, he was Portuguese. Then she asked if he would return to Portugal at the end of the war.

In certain situations and circumstances feelings and dreams take an infinite time to take shape. At other times they are born, develop and mature in but a few hours. Each of them soon realized that if they kept up this retreat day and night all the way to Madrid, it wouldn't be long before they would seek a new outlet for their affection. *Surely, surely, she will be mine.* António was unable to banish the idea. And his thinking spun ever longer into the future, daring to contradict reality. *After we get to Madrid, if she wants it, I'll make her my companion, and after the war we'll go to Portugal.*

Things did not go as he imagined foolishly. After two days in the fugitive cortege, the course of events took an abrupt turn.

Heading in the same direction, a truck rumbled in with a bunch of armed militiamen. The refugees stopped to look. On the road blocked by the multitude came a rainstorm of questions and news.

The fascists had occupied the border, taking villages, assassinating populations *en masse*. The group was going to Madrid to relate the situation and ask for reinforcements.

António ran through the crowd, making his way toward the truck. So that they would recognize in him a fellow combatant, he placed the holster of his revolver in plain view, up until then covered by the hem of his shirt.

"Hey, guys!" he shouted. "Can I go with you?"

They asked who he was.

"I'm Portuguese, I was out here with a column that got wiped out on the road to Badajoz."

They didn't believe him. "Everybody's got their story. Go back to your people and follow along with them."

The driver honked the horn repeatedly to clear the way. The crowd had already parted and moved to the edges of the road when one of the men on the truck broke with his mates and started shouting for the driver to stop. António heard the cries of "Stop! Stop!" and saw the guy's arms waving. Only then did he see one face stand out from the rest as it turned toward him. It was Rubio, the *compañero* with whom he had traveled with the column precisely to Badajoz and whom he hadn't seen since that night when the Carlists occupied the village and he had jumped shoeless from the truck. So he had saved himself! How, António didn't know yet.

Rubio spoke with the others, they told António to get on, and they helped him clamber up.

António climbed up as fast as he could, the truck's motor spurted faster as it accelerated, and only then did he realize that he hadn't said goodbye to his companions of the road, not even to Celia. He almost tried to get off the truck and go back. But then it lurched forward, heaving one against another in this pack of armed men thrust together. From the bed of the truck he made one desperate gesture of goodbye. *Adiós*. The girl answered with a gesture of her own, resigned and sad. And that was it.

8

A few kilometers ahead they accessed the main highway. From time to time they passed trucks and cars going in the other direction, some flying their banners, armed volunteers going to the front as reinforcements.

Also every once in a while, heading north, they passed small processions of civilians with mules and loaded carts. Surely they were fleeing from the fascist advance.

Along the way Rubio recounted how he had escaped. Like António, he had been sleeping when the fascists entered the village. Many of the *compañeros* had no time to move into defensive positions, or even to offer a show of defense. They were instantly killed. He and a couple of others managed to grab their weapons and put up some resistance. It was all he could do, though, to escape into the fields and run away. He did not know the fate of the others. Only one other escaped with him. "That guy there!" and he pointed to a hefty man squatting in the truck, sleeping profoundly, his head bent to one side.

They arrived in Madrid in late afternoon. António went right to the house. Only Madrecita was home.

"What happened, *hijo mío?*" she exclaimed, seeing his lamentable state. "Come here, let me take care of you."

"Manuel?" he asked. "Eulalia?" Manuel had not returned again. Eulalia hadn't been around for some time. António insisted he didn't have much time. He wanted to leave right away, and they could talk later.

"Leave in the condition you're in? What you need is to take care of yourself!"

She helped him to wash up and attend to his sunburned face and his swollen, lacerated feet. She brought him fresh, clean clothes. And gave him bread with sausage that he swallowed almost in a gulp without chewing.

"Everything's all right, my son," she concluded. "But you shouldn't go out yet. There'll be time tomorrow. What's the rush?" Then she added, "I understand, it's your duty. But can't you wait until tomorrow?"

António hurried to The Comrade's house to give him an account of his mission. In the area around Badajoz, where in better times cross-border passage was safer, the frontier had been occupied by fascist troops. Crossing there would not be possible.

"If you can't cross there," The Comrade said, "you can't cross anywhere. The whole frontier with Portugal is in their hands."

He did not ask how things had gone. It was obvious. For him the result was what mattered. The negative answer posed new, serious problems. If the border was closed and yet he still needed to return to Portugal, how would he do it? "We have to find some other solution. Now it's back in your pocket."

That was all. Their very brief meeting ended.

The Comrade had clearly summarized the essence of the mission, that the possibility of returning to Portugal overland was not viable, and that they needed to find some other way.

But what the hell! Everything António had gone through was of no interest? Didn't count for anything? He had come back—and if he hadn't? Is that the way to treat your cadres? Prepare yourself, go out, risk your life, die if that's what happens, what's important is the result? In this case, a negative result and the need to find another way. No, there was something wrong with this picture. There was no appreciation and respect for the comrades, not even for the human being, that's what it is!"

The next day he saw he didn't have quite enough cause to think in that way. The Comrade called him to his house and had him sit down. "So, tell me how everything went."

António began his account and they talked for a long time. But that would be the next day. Now, he went back to

Eulalia's house, not inspired by the righteous satisfaction of having completed his assignment and acquitting himself well, but still, offended by the dry objectivity with which he was received.

Madrecita, worried about António's state of mind having just returned from a meeting, was relieved to see him back sooner than she expected.

She had prepared a *tortilla*. "Eat, eat!" she repeated, seeing the way he hungrily devoured the dish. "Eat, son, you need to eat."

After he finished, they talked. She said once again she knew nothing about Eulalia. Her daughter had come to the house only once. Yes, in a black uniform, with a pistol at her waist, and white shoes with black ribbons tied around the ankles. Very military. At the same time, with her loose black hair, her beautiful arms, a liveliness all her own, she had lost nothing of her feminine grace.

And Manuel? Yes, he showed up a couple of times, armed, and headed right back out to Guadarrama. She didn't know exactly where.

António didn't hear those last words. He suddenly passed out, and his head fell forward to the table until his forehead reached the wood. Madrecita didn't wake him up. She got a pillow and raised his head to place it under his face. She pulled his arms up to the table and stayed by his side, sitting watchfully.

Chapter V

1

A few days later, António had just come from a chat with The Comrade. At the Socorro, he met Rubio, who grabbed him by the arm. "I'm going to see how my little sister works," and he indicated the revolver he had on his belt. "Come with me. I want to see your aim that you put to such good use on your retreat from our expedition."

António had recounted his tribulations on the trip, the boots he'd had to take from the farmer and the intimidation he had to exercise, all thanks to his revolver, the weighty, shining Smith 32. He accepted the invitation with delight.

They had repurposed several areas of the immense building. In one part, beyond the gate and the sizable entrance patio, and extending out into the cloister and the wide corridors, the field hospital was already functioning. In another wing, with exits to the side streets and to the rear of the building, they created a huge space to receive refugees and the concentration of various militia units.

In the basement of that area they had installed a place reserved for those responsible for security and defense of the building. From that locale volunteers set out for the Fifth Regiment, where they received military training before being sent to the front lines. There they kept and received weapons, and handed out ammunition according to need and the orders of the military committee in charge of the armed support groups. Arms experts went there to inspect the weapons, clean and prime them for firing, and even make small repairs. Rounding out that section was what they ironically called the "firing range," a long passage at the end of which they had placed targets.

The two friends descended to the basement to try it out.

First, Rubio fired one, two, three shots multiplying and banking the echoes against the cellar walls. One bullet hit the bullseye, the other two hit the first circle.

Then António. "You'll see!" he said gaily as he aimed. Surprise! They heard the snap of the trigger, a second snap and yet a third.

"Shit, what's going on?" he cursed and pulled back the firing pin to see if the bullets were in place, which they were. He aimed again, squeezed the trigger, and nothing.

Looking once more, they found another surprise. This magnificent Smith 32 revolver, which had played such a significant role on his trip, had a cracked firing pin!

2

Having obtained a new weapon, António faced another issue of a technical nature. Transportation in the city was disorganized. He and his comrades had to get around. They lived far from one another, so they had to get a car. It wasn't that difficult. The popular forces' cars that circulated around the city by the hundreds were almost all "requisitioned." You had to requisition one even for your own employment. Just mulling over the problem wouldn't do—he had to act, and so he did.

That's when the memory came into his head of the automobile repair shop where he had worked and to which he never went back. The guys there possibly could give him some useful information. He would start there.

Old Bártolo and Ramón welcomed him exuberantly. "*Chico*, what have you been up to all this time? We thought you were either dead or in Portugal."

"There's a war. I'm in it," António responded.

His two companions told him that the other guys working there had also left. There was nothing to do now in the little shop, and they were considering closing it.

As for the question António posed—where was the best place to requisition a car—they mentioned a big collection garage in the central zone of the city.

António had already said his goodbyes and exited when Ramón called after him, "Hey, what about your cycle?"

Strange as it might seem, António, who before had gathered crowds and excited the enthusiasm of anyone passing by with his speed and acrobatics, had not even remembered the motorcycle he had left in the shop for repair after an accident.

Ramón's words evoked a sudden thunderbolt of memory and feeling—the noisy roar of the engine, the strong vibration passing through the steering handles into the palms of his hands, the contained energy poised to unleash and then, releasing the tension, the scream of the machine, the lurch forward and his body tearing through space and air like a cyclone caressing his face and his hair standing up and flying back.

"It's damaged—beyond repair," he answered and left.

That afternoon he asked Renato to accompany him to the big collection garage that his coworkers had spoken of.

The man in charge of the garage helped them. He showed no surprise seeing them both with a weapon on their belt. From the way they approached him, he clearly guessed why they had come.

António went straight to the point with no pussyfooting around. "Listen, *compañero*, don't you have a car here for us?"

Certainly we do, the manager immediately answered. Dozens of them. *Belonging to fascists who've fled from the capital or who are hiding defeated and terrified in a hole somewhere.* He did not actually say that, but it's what he wanted to say.

"What car do you want?" he asked, as the three men strolled down the rows of parked cars.

António hadn't thought about it. "Well, one we can use—"

"Can you use that one?" and the manager pointed to a beautiful red convertible.

António picked up on the mischievous undertone. "You want them to shoot us first thing?"

"And this one?" It was a small, discolored old Austin.

"Enough with the jokes," António shot at him, not appreciating his humor.

The manager switched topics. "Requisitioned? By whom?"

"By the International Red Aid," António quickly answered.

The manager kept his silence as they walked further.

"This one will do." António pointed to a small car with four seats and an innocuous appearance.

"You can take it," the manager consented. But once António had turned the motor on, the manager added, "Be careful, *chico*. You didn't want the other one, but they could shoot you for this one too."

Only later did António pick up on what the jokester intended, exactly because the car had that discreet, anonymous look about it. But it was a high-priced automobile, a Lancia that belonged to some moneybags now either a refugee or dead.

With the car requisitioned, he had to get it running. For one thing, it wouldn't be only António driving it.

"Do you want to learn?" he proposed to Renato.

"Okay," is all the comrade said.

They set a day, hour and place and met there. "It's covered with dust, we'd better wash it," Renato suggested.

"Don't even think about it, *amigo*." António had reflected on what the garage manager had told him as they parted. "Just clean the windows. With all the dust they won't see what kind of car it is."

In fact, covered in dust, it did not look like a pricey model but an old, worn-out car.

António gave Renato a quick round of explanations and put him at the wheel. He marveled at Renato's ability as he turned the motor on, accelerated a little to get it running steady, pressed on the clutch, put the car in first, let up the brakes, stepped on the gas pedal and started off with no problem, just one abrupt spurt as they started, nothing more. Switching from first to second and from second to third, he managed the road well.

"You already knew how to drive," António protested.
"No, no, I didn't."
"Dammit, don't try to fool me, you knew!"
Renato didn't repeat himself; he just shrugged his shoulders.

He made only slight mistakes, a little grinding as he switched gears, and one curve that he took too wide. The next day they had another lesson and the teacher explained a few more details.

3

Now they were ready to take the car out of the city. They had been informed that, on the Republican lines at Guadarrama, a Portuguese had been taken prisoner on suspicion of giving signals to the enemy. He said he was a Communist.

"Not possible!" António said indignantly, recalling that Manuel was there on the front lines and he was the only Portuguese they knew about on that front. "This is a *compañero* I have complete confidence in," he stated when he heard the news.

Well, they had to go, and get there fast, because on the front lines summary judgment reigned. They quickly obtained credentials allowing them to go to the front.

Did he have transportation to get there? Yes, now he had a car—proof of how necessary and correct it was to requisition the Lancia. Completely necessary and correct. Who would dare object?

He took Renato along to accompany him. Right at the Socorro door who should show up in front of them making them stop but Barata! Motioning excitedly, he shouted his request: "Can I go with you?"

Surely he had been watching them and listening to their conversation. One could only guess why. António had never spoken with him. He had only seen him once or twice, and that was well before the Popular Front victory, and then again, not long before, standing in the street. Well dressed and wearing a tie, shameless in whatever he was mixed up with, he would speak of business he was involved in and was not well received by the Portuguese exiles. Now he showed up quite by surprise, less the dandy than usual, and with this strange request.

No, António answered coldly, he could not take him. His name was not listed on the credentials.

"It doesn't matter, I have a *carnet* —a pass from the Republican Party."

"That won't do—"

"What do you mean that won't do? I'm a member of the Republican Party, not the Portuguese party, but the Spanish party, which is in the government," and with that he shoved his arm through the car window with the *carnet* in his hand so that António could see.

"All right! We'll soon see, get in," he conceded, undone.

Outside Madrid, a zigzag barricade to control traffic blocked the highway. A huge red and black diagonal flag indicated the anarchists. A lot of them were there, many wearing their caps with the slanted red and black. They made the car stop and, brandishing rifles in front of them, asked for documents. The Party credentials did not satisfy them. They wanted to know more.

"These credentials are for two. We can't allow three to go through."

From the back seat, Barata entered the conversation. "Here is my *carnet*. I am a member of the Socialist Party of Spain."

The anarchist took the document, and looked at it with a slight smile, returning it without comment. He took a few steps back, then returned. "Three Portuguese? What are you going to do there?"

What the credentials say, António answered without further explanation. He didn't have to explain, he thought. Besides, if he said they were going to clear up the situation of a Portuguese suspected of making signals to the enemy, they wouldn't allow them to pass. But it wasn't only that. The credentials also didn't specify anything except to certify that it had to do with *compañeros* on a party mission.

They were held there a good half hour for no reason. The men at the post circulated around them and observed them, sometimes whispering amongst themselves in a joking attitude. It was obvious they weren't doing anything useful but had just decided to annoy them.

Renato casually smoked a cigarette. Barata, seated in back, kept quiet. António, though impatient, restrained himself. Finally one of the men at the barricade came to the car window and without saying a word made a gesture with his hand for them to proceed.

4

António stopped the Lancia on the open highway and got out.
"Renato, you drive!"
"Me?!"
"Yes, you."
Renato was surprised—two lessons were very few—but he didn't protest.
The two got out to trade places, and António whispered to his companion, "Did you notice? In Madrid he showed us his Republican Party *carnet*. Here he showed one from the Socialist Party. I do not like our company."
Renato assumed the wheel and they took off for the mountains. While the highway was flat, all went well. On the straightaways their speed increased to more than 80 kilometers an hour, leaving a cloud of dust in their wake.
"You drive well," Barata said appreciatively. "You have style."
"He's an ace!" António confirmed. "I see you know what you're talking about, Senhor Barata."
Renato noted the irony, having had two lessons only days before. Calmly concentrating on the road, he didn't react to the humor.
"It's a fact," Barata agreed from the back seat, his hands now grasping the back of the seat in front of him by way of continuing the conversation.
When they started going up the mountain, things changed markedly—ever more potholes, the road steeper, more curves and narrower passages. As they made their ascent, the noise of gunshots echoing through the hills heightened the background sound.
On the narrowest curves the car started to drift out of control toward the other side of the road or skid from the

sudden braking. At one point, rolling off on its own, it wound up stopped at the edge on the other side with the hood perched over a ravine.

"Bravo!" an amused António cried. "I wouldn't have been able to do that!"

Barata, in a state of existential shock, still wanted not to make the worst of it. "This is just acrobatics now. But weren't you going too fast?"

"No way! An ace is an ace!" António teased Renato, but Renato didn't play the victim. "You know something?" António asked, turning around toward the back seat. "Do you know how many years our friend has had his driver's license?"

"To drive that way, obviously many years," Barata had to grant.

The car skidded once more and António replied with a guffaw, now addressing him without the honorific "Senhor." "Years? Can you believe it, *chico*, I myself taught him to drive just two days ago."

"No!" Barata protested.

"Seriously, two days ago—"

At that moment the car made a tremendous noise. The squeal of the tires mixed with the now intense sound of machine gunning that coursed throughout the mountain range.

Now Barata was seriously in shock. "Are you guys crazy or what!?" He wanted to make his voice sound overpowering but it came out trembling, hoarse and strained.

Every time the driver demonstrated his insecurity at the wheel, Barata shouted out and shifted anxiously in his seat. Stop this foolishness! We're going to crash! We're on a serious mission! We're not here to take idiotic risks!

The jokes stopped. But until they arrived at the first military checkpoint, Renato never took his foot off the accelerator, and neither did António ask him to slow down.

5

They showed their credentials, but this was just a preliminary inspection. Two or three kilometers farther on they showed their papers again and explained why they had come. The soldiers told them to leave their car and follow the path up to another post a few hundred meters higher.

António couldn't contain himself. "If it's the *compañero* I think it is, I know him very well. He came to Spain having already fought against fascism in Portugal—"

The Spaniards interrupted him. "Things are not so clear, *compañero*. They caught him among the rocks directly across from the enemy lines, raising his flashlight above his head, giving signals—"

"That's impossible," António objected.

"Very well, talk with him. He's not far from here under watch. Talk with him, then we'll talk. Albertino, take the *compañero* there."

The three Portuguese started to follow. "No!" the Spaniard quickly interceded. "Just you, you go alone!"

After taking a few pathways to get there, António stood in front of a cave with two militiamen at the entrance.

"Bring the prisoner," ordered Albertino. In an instant the prisoner came out of the cave.

"Oh!" António exclaimed. It was not Manuel! It was a youth—very young—pale, short, dressed in rags, squinting his eyes at the intense brightness of the sun at that height in the mountains.

Embarrassed by his wrong judgment that it was Manuel, António explained that the prisoner was not the person he believed it would be, but he would talk with him and then report. "All right, talk," the militiaman said.

Looking at him close-up, he saw the youth was even younger than he seemed at first. The boy was Portuguese. He said he had come to the sierra with a group of militiamen who had seen him as they passed by and invited him to join them. They didn't give him a weapon, and he found himself on the front lines alongside combatants sheltered from the gunfire by boulders. Once night had closed in, he figured he would take advantage of an opening and decided to leave there and return to Madrid. If he weren't armed, what was he doing at the front? He filched a flashlight and tried to escape lighting the uneven terrain when they jumped on him, seized him and accused him of sending light signals to the fascists.

The more he insisted on his story, the more the comrades doubted it. For one thing, he wasn't walking back to the rear but toward the fascist lines, as the Spanish militiaman continued to emphasize.

"Bullshit, *compañero*! How do you expect him to know the route?" said António in exasperation.

They kept their peace. If he didn't believe it, he didn't believe it, what could they do?

"All right," António addressed the boy, "who are you?"

The boy explained that he lived with his family in Madrid. They were from Sabugal, and his father worked in civil construction.

"What's your name?"

"Raul," the boy answered. He gave off no signs of anxiousness from what was happening.

"I'll see what I can do," António promised. And he translated his conversation to the Spaniards.

"He's only a child, *compañeros*. You're not going to kill him, are you? You can't. He's a child."

They told him to talk to the lieutenant.

Luckily, they found him at the post by the entrance to the path. The lieutenant was a combatant like the others, a strong man, grizzled face, shirtsleeves rolled up, dusty shoes, pistol worn over his shoulder.

It could be just as the kid says, but at the front you always have to keep your eyes open. Two men had already deserted to the enemy. Anyone who wants to comes to the front, and those guys had come too, in fact with the lieutenant himself and others. And what happened? In the end they came just trying to escape from Madrid and pass themselves off. At this moment, he couldn't decide anything.

"He's a child," António insisted. "It would be a crime to kill him."

"I think like you, *compañero*. No one's considering killing him. That's why we asked Madrid for someone to come—a Portuguese, of course."

The sound of gunfire was growing ever louder. On top of the rattle from the rifles and machine guns, at that moment came the prolonged, deafening sound of cannon shots.

"They're attacking!" the lieutenant exclaimed.

António tried to insist, but the lieutenant cut the conversation short. He had to drop everything and go where he was needed. As he ran off, he only added that António should try and confirm in Madrid what the boy had told about his family. "If it's true, come back tomorrow. I'll expect you."

6

The return trip to Madrid did not go smoothly. Not on account of Renato's crazy driving, because António drove, but because of new surprises en route.

A dense net of gunshots from every kind of weapon spread through the mountain air, under which thrummed a constant echoing—and echoing of echoing. From time to time, muffled but dominating, came the distinct thundering of cannons.

Not far from the front, on a curvy hillside atop a deep valley, the car was moving along at a good clip when a sharp whistle passed through the air, and right in front of them, a few dozen meters ahead, came the glare and explosion of a grenade. In the back seat Barata grunted. António braked abruptly, the smell of burnt metal arose, and the car wound up at the edge of the road.

António anxiously looked down at the precipice all too near them, right in front of the car.

Renato was first to get out. "Let's do it!"

The others got out too. Barata, of a deadly pallor, had lost the will to speak. The three pushed the car back onto the road, and they started off again.

Then another whistle, another sudden braking and a little farther up, on the curb itself, the flash of light, the cloud of dust and fire, and the deafening boom of a grenade.

"This is ugly!" said António, his hands gripping the steering wheel.

"What are you waiting for?" Renato spoke up uncharacteristically. "Don't stop, speed up!"

They got to Madrid without further incident. Only Barata felt the need to say something on his own behalf. "I'd go back to the front a thousand times, but never again with lunatics."

"I can assure you, you're not going back a thousand times," said António, not disguising his sense of irony. "And I doubt you'll ever go back, not even once."

The boy taken prisoner at Guadarrama had spoken the truth. They found the family in the house he had indicated. It was a middle-aged Portuguese couple who had been working in Spain for years. They were anxious because their son had disappeared from home.

"He's a jerk," the father said. "A screw loose. Doesn't know enough to stay home."

The next day António and Renato went back to the mountain. The lieutenant was waiting for them and felt pleased and relieved. He took leave of the boy with an affectionate knock on his arm. "Be careful, *amigo.*"

They brought the boy back to Madrid. The fascist attempt to advance failed. Just a few dispersed shots were heard. The return trip occurred uneventfully. António resumed his bright, optimistic manner of seeing things. On the way he got to talking with the boy, half seriously and half joking. "Did you learn anything from your scare, eh?"

"Not really," the boy answered, as if nothing had happened.

7

The necessity and usefulness of the requisitioned car had been quickly proven. The car was good, fast, comfortable and of modest appearance. Among friends, António bragged of his success. Now he could come and go from the house two or more times a day. If called for, he could see anyone he wanted without waiting for messages or spending hours walking. He could take comrades home after meetings. He could even seek out the Hotel Berne Group for a meeting.

He decided to take the good news to Fernando Torres, who received him cordially as always. They talked about the situation, and António offered to transport him if he ever needed it.

In the middle of their conversation, a young man entered the room. Clean-cut, well-dressed, he shook hands enthusiastically.

"This is Abel, my son," Fernando Torres introduced him.

António knew of his existence, but this was the first time António had met him. Before the coup took place he had come from Portugal, where he was studying, to spend his vacation with his parents. He was also caught off guard by the war, and had remained in Madrid.

Instantly, António saw how Abel resembled his father. Not only physically, but in his manner and the unpretentious, confident way he addressed other people. *If you pasted a wispy beard on his face, he'd look just like his father*, António thought.

"So what have you been doing? How has it gone for you during all this?" he asked the young man.

He hadn't gone out the first day and he avoided areas with gunfire, but he was excited. He'd been seeing things and learning. "How lucky that I'm here with the unique opportunity to witness a revolution. They're extraordinary human beings, the Spanish people."

Further in the conversation António asked him what he was considering doing.

"The same as I've been—"

"Nothing?"

"What do you mean, nothing? Learning is doing something."

"Listen, *amigo*," said Fernando, smiling and in good spirits. "Now that you've met Abel, you won't want to be recruiting him to the party. Let the boy explore more and choose for himself."

Let him explore, let him explore, António thought. But what if he himself was "exploring?" Well, that's a longer story for another time, and it wasn't what had brought him to the Torres house.

"Do you know how to drive a car?" he asked, already standing and ready to leave.

"No, I don't know. Right now I'm not interested," Fernando stated.

"I could teach you."

The news was given, the offer made—to Fernando and to his son.

He left and on touching the steering wheel he felt satisfaction with the good thinking that led him to requisition a car. Even more a Lancia, that Lancia.

8

His good luck didn't last long.

Rubio was getting ready to depart once again in the direction of Badajoz, now occupied by the fascists. The news had spread. On August 14th they had slaughtered, machine gunned hundreds and hundreds of civilians they'd forcibly rounded up into the bull ring. Now he wasn't going there just to assess the situation and report back, but to stay there and join the Republican forces who were opposing the fascist advance.

They got into the Lancia, and António drove Rubio around on various errands he had to attend to. Then Rubio asked him if he could loan him the car that night for an outing of a very personal nature. He would leave it in the same spot, at the Socorro door.

"It's yours," António agreed, happy to be able to loan it to his friend.

The next morning the car wasn't there. When he asked the comrades, they told him that Rubio's column had left the night before and that he had left a letter for António. It read:

"António, my dear *compañero*. I'm going to the front. There are no cars there. You're staying in Madrid, where there are many. I know you can buy one for the same price this one cost. Thank you with all my heart. Your comrade and friend always, Rubio."

He could have gotten angry. But no. He found it amusing and, unlike his habit in recent times, he even thought in Portuguese: "*What a bastard!*" And he laughed to himself, able to appreciate the parting trick.

Renato did not think much of the story. "You trusted, now you've learned."

The way he saw things, António did not look back. He imagined the column marching under better circumstances. The situation in Madrid could be fixed today.

That afternoon António and Renato returned to the huge collection garage and found the manager.

"Hey, *compañero*, is there an available car anywhere?"

"Yes, many, which one do you want?"

"A Lancia if there is one." He demonstrably loved the one Rubio took.

The manager had a good memory. "You're the one who took the Lancia. I warned you that on account of the Lancia they'd kill you. I'm happy you escaped. And now, what would you like? Will a Cadillac do? Or do you prefer a Rolls Royce?"

António joked: "I can see you wish for my death, *amigo*. If they find me in a Cadillac they'll take me for a millionaire and will shoot me."

Continuing his joshing around, he pointed to a handsome Lincoln. "And this one? Can I take it?"

"No," the manager cut him off. "The Lincoln is for the Socialists. They like nice cars. It will be their undoing."

And now in all seriousness he showed them a black Citroën, their *Traction Avant* model with front wheel drive. "This one you can take. The owner's not coming back." And he amiably added, "Besides, it's a good car and the tank is full." He went to get the keys and handed them over.

The two comrades got in and turned the ignition on. "*Gracias, compañero, uachepé!*" and took off.

The next day, Renato found António in an alley behind the Socorro brushing the Citroën door with yellow paint. He drew closer.

"Do you like it?" António asked. On the door, plainly visible, he had painted a hammer and sickle and PCP. "Rubio ought to get a look at this!"

And he laughed imagining the scene that awaited them when their friend would return and see António's masterpiece.

9

How was it possible for António to imagine that the Portuguese arrested on suspicion at Guadarrama was Manuel? Simply because Guadarrama and Manuel fighting at Guadarrama were inseparable thoughts. Because he had seen Manuel's courage close-up, and dreaded every day that he'd lose his life there.

But no, because such a thing could never happen to Manuel. Because since the earliest days of combat, he was on the most forward lines. Because he was always showing proof of his initiative and bravery. Because he was beloved of his Spanish comrades, with whom he successfully restrained the fascist efforts at that mountain to break a path through to Madrid.

On the very first day he had participated in the attack on the Cuartel de la Montaña and was among those who busted inside through the gate to put an end—with bullets—to the last acts of resistance by the rebel officers.

Then at Carabanchel, when he advanced with António and the swell of an armed citizenry, seeing how the fascist machine gunners' niche had borne up under attack, the idea came to him suddenly and instinctively. They were not advancing on that side. They wouldn't succeed, except by attacking the fascists at their rear. And he started running, trying to survive the open space where a crossfire of bullets was flying. He even surprised himself with his success. Descending more and more, describing a long arc along the hillside, he saw he was facing an empty terrain and, a little above and with their backs to him, with no rearguard support, the group of four or five fascists firing their machine gun. His Mauser was a puny weapon by contrast. The psychological factor would be decisive. Manuel impressed himself by the speed with which he took stock of the situation and decided his strategy. *When they see they're being attacked from the rear, they'll run away*, he surmised. He crept up, got nearer and aimed. Amidst the crashing din of battle thundering throughout the mountains, his two rifle shots were not even heard. Next to their machine gun, struck by his bullets, two bodies fell. The crackle of machine gunning ceased, and the survivors of the group, abandoning arms, ran desperately toward their barracks.

An advance down the hillside beckoned him irresistibly. Manuel lost sight of the young boy who had stuck close by him, and also could no longer see António and the others in his group. For sure, they had stayed well behind. He continued his approach along with many others from all directions who emerged from their hiding places. He was among those on the front lines, fraternizing with the soldiers loyal to the Republic, who forced the rebel officers to surrender.

He returned to Madrid in a parade of the large victorious column integrated into a group of young Spanish fighters with whom he had shared the final assault. With Pablo, with Jaime, with Alonso, with Consuelo. Like hundreds of others, that combat group had been born, constituted and acted as a military unit that very morning. That one morning they had shielded one another always attentive to the enemy and to the action and danger their companions were risking. They conquered the enemy and they conquered death that hovered over them without pity. And now Pablo, Jaime, Alonso, Consuelo, Manuel looked at each other as lifelong friends, and as though they could never be separated.

10

Together they had returned to Madrid with the triumphant forces of Carabanchel. Unlike many who dispersed, these five never separated from the popular armed forces. Where this feeling came from no one could say. One thing was certain for them and for thousands of other combatants. Someone had joined them to the military column that left for Guadarrama to cut off the fascists' path as they advanced from the north. Integrating themselves into the column, they were no longer merely five friends who had come together in combat. They were truly—and they felt it as well—a military cell of the new army, the people's army in formation from that day on.

They and hundreds of others were brought directly to the most advanced lines in the sierra. Among them, surely someone knew the terrain and commanded the deployment of the forces. But once they were in the sierra, however, each person on their own took the initiative to choose their own position.

Manuel and his companions, among many others, were brought to a high rocky outcropping overlooking a long valley with a road snaking through it.

The mission was simple. To prevent the fascist advance by that road, there were other units, with other equipment, which could not be seen from there. These had artillery, machine guns and mortars. Here the objective was different. It was to prevent the fascists, advancing through the mountains, from gaining positions dominating the valley or being able to attack Republican troops at their rear.

The foresight was justified. In those first few days, battles raged all throughout the sierra.

Manuel, Pablo, Alonso, Jaime, Consuelo, acted like a combat unit. They were venturesome and functioned with a high degree of mutual assistance.

One time Manuel was left isolated in an exposed position. And it was Pablo and Alonso who, at great risk, taking dangerous positions, held the fascists down and gave Manuel cover.

Another time it was Manuel who saw his companions in a perilous situation. The fascists had gained positions on a higher terrain and were firing from above. At that moment the memory came to Manuel of the Public Fair in Lisbon, the comrades passing out leaflets and he, assuring their defense, attacking the policeman who had arrested them. As at Carabanchel, the initiative appeared naturally and effortlessly. Here it was a question of gaining a position higher on the terrain than that of the fascists, from there dominating them and forcing them to fire in his direction, thus opening up space for Pablo and Alonso to escape.

They fought as a team, not even thinking about death, almost even seeming to toy with it. But in war, death lurks and strikes mercilessly. In the very first days at Guadarrama the group suffered a hard blow. Consuelo, the young woman who had joined them at Carabanchel, who with rifle in hand had advanced with them on the final attack on the garrison, who there at Guadarrama always sought out the front lines and the biggest risks, a heroine of the group and beloved by all, fell in open combat.

After two weeks, as his companions also did, Manuel rotated and returned to Madrid to rest a while, to eat some good meals, to wash up, maybe shave, and once refreshed, return to the sierra. In other words, concretely speaking, to go to the house where he felt at home, to catch up with António, Renato and the others, to see Madrecita. And also, needless to say, to see Eulalia.

11

This time it was Eulalia who opened the door. A tight, long embrace followed. He released from it slowly and looked straight at her.

"Good, you're alive," she told him.

Madrecita joined them in the dining room. "Give me a kiss too, *hijo*."

They exchanged news. Manuel said only that he'd been at the front and referred to his companions. He reported just the result of the combat without further description. He spoke little of himself, and then was quiet.

"You're alive, that's what counts," Eulalia concluded. And she related her news. She had more responsibilities now, not only in the neighborhood but in the city. She was organizing another field hospital, but was not happy staying back on the home front.

Madrecita said that António now only rarely showed up. And when he did stop by, he hardly spoke. He took a bath, shaved and left. She didn't know exactly what he was doing. Eulalia had also seen him one of those times. There was something that struck her. "You know?" she said to Manuel, "I don't see that special happiness of his any more. He seems like a man who goes around looking for the path toward death."

Madrecita went to bed. The two remained talking in the most general of terms—the ferociousness of the enemy, the armed response from the people, accidents, stories. But apart from these events and happenings, something subtle, imperceptible and enveloping was taking shape and taking hold of the conversation. Eulalia peered into Manuel's young face, the firm lines, the skin browned by the sun, the thin, silky beard waiting to be shaved, into his earnest eyes and direct gaze. Manuel didn't run away—and why would he?—from the pleasure of enjoying the captivating beauty of the woman he held before him in his eyes. He saw a figure of harmonious form, dark, intense, resolute, a delicate face and loving eyes adorned by her black hair and the fine shape of her lips that, when she pronounced certain words and when she smiled, showed off one twisted tooth out of alignment that lent her a unique grace.

They continued talking, unhurriedly, running out of topics. Maybe for Madrecita to sleep peacefully, they kept their voices low, almost to a whisper.

"Okay, it's time for bed," he said.

They stood up, Eulalia lazily, with the pretense of a stretch, Manuel never allowing his eyes to let go of her.

"Get some rest," she said.

From the next room came Madrecita's quavering snore. From some indeterminate place outside came the sound of occasional gunshots.

"Are you going back to Guadarrama?"

"Yes, to the front at Somosierra."

"I want you alive, you know."

"I want you alive too."

"Yes, I know that."

Chapter VI

1

DAY after day caravans of refugees flooded into the capital. The fascist troops had let loose a furious storm of atrocious attacks, raping women, pillaging villages, shooting at random. They had advanced to Talavera de la Reina and the Toledo region, not far from Madrid.

The rural population hurriedly bundled up as much as they could, equipped their pack animals and hitched their burros or horses to their carts, taking with them everything possible and, except for a few who stayed behind to put up some resistance and give themselves more time to retreat, commenced their journey to the capital.

Across the faraway countryside groups of refugees calculated their itinerary by paths and roads, converging and amassing until they joined together on the principal highways in great human chains, now distant from the combat zones.

Volunteers at the Socorro tried to welcome them, find them shelter and get them something to eat. But more and more kept coming, piling up in the courtyard of the building or, given the nighttime heat, in the open air on the sidewalk outside.

António carefully surveyed each new group as they arrived, hoping to recognize someone amongst them— especially one—with whom he had marched in the retreat from Badajoz. A few, he did. More than once amid the human mass it seemed he had found the figure, the profile, the mannerisms or the kerchief of Celia, the dark girl who was his companion on that strenuous march. What might have happened? Where could she be?

Renato also saw throngs of refugees every day. Now he was in the enormous building where he was taken by Pepe, one of the Spanish *compañeros* he had been with on the Gran Vía. Just as he had integrated himself into a combat group, now he was in a group of armed guards at the field hospital.

There, at the street-level gate, he encountered António. It was almost unimaginable: Renato, peaceable Renato, who didn't want to get mixed up in troubles, but who nevertheless did so in the sniping, on the Gran Vía, at the sierra, stood there, natural, authentic, self-possessed, with a rifle at his shoulder.

"You here? What a surprise! What are you doing now, *amigo*?"

Very simple: He was with the security guard at the hospital. With what unit? Just the hospital guard, nothing more. We have shifts, he added.

"So for you it's arms yes, but armed struggle no?"

"Here I'm useful," Renato answered. "The war is for them."

2

On his guard shift, Renato circulated throughout the hospital. He marveled that such a hospital had materialized out of so many different good intentions. The young nurses, the doctors, the stretcher bearers, the cleaning staff, the armed security group, constituted a huge collective dedicated to effectively fulfilling their responsibilities. Renato felt bound to each and every one of them, his *compañeros*.

With one exception. He specifically did not like the hospital director, Tó Marcolino. No one could say who had chosen him for the position, nor what his knowledge and experience consisted of. No one even knew for sure what his profession was, nor where he got such a name. But in the spontaneous combustion of many personalities that led to the creation of the hospital, he was the one who emerged to direct it all, and he stayed on.

Some said that owing to him, his work and his iron hand, the hospital in all its complexity was able to function. Nevertheless, Renato observed some strange behavior.

There was, for example, the plenary session Marcolino convoked for all the nursing personnel. For what? To impose discipline in the relationships between nurses and the hospitalized wounded, not allowing for any intimacies. He did not limit himself to establishing norms and to making his speech. With the accusatory rigor of a judge, he pointed a finger at Angelita, a rather shy young woman, pronouncing his sentence. "It's over, Angelita. You're getting into bed with the wounded patients. It's over now, we don't want you here. It's over."

And as the woman broke into tears, and a light murmur of disapproval ran through the plenary, a voice could be heard: "She didn't want anything to do with *you*, right?"

Everyone heard this comment. But not everyone heard another, this one not directed to Marcolino. In a quiet voice it was directed by one participant in the session to another. "Dr. Lorenzo can now feel reassured. The director fires the girls who go to bed with the wounded, not the ones who go with the doctors."

Another incident heightened the antipathy and reservations Renato had for the director. It took place in the cloister, when Tó Marcolino crossed in front of Renato. "Hey, *amigo*, what are you doing here?"

Renato did not care for his attitude, but he explained what he was doing. The explanation appeared to provoke the director's anger. He started shouting at him and wouldn't stop, in a literal act of denunciation. "Portuguese? And why are you Portuguese helping the Spanish people? You're not doing anything here. Are you just hoping we'll win the war and then go liberate you from Salazar? They're organizing International Brigades. The German are coming, the French,

Italians, Russians, Czechs. But we don't hear anything about the Portuguese."

Renato listened to everything he said, but showed no reaction—no words, no gestures, no expression.

"So, what do you have to say?" the director went on, even more aggressively.

Renato made no response and continued on his way into the cloister.

Tó Marcolino kept shouting, trying to order Renato to come back, but without effect.

Renato told António about it, and António spoke to Gonzalo, whose reaction was not much to his credit. "You're right, Marcolino was not proper. It's true, but that's just his way. You can't take what he says seriously."

That's all? António wanted to discuss the incident, yes, in all seriousness. But he restrained himself and didn't respond, just like Renato with Tó Marcolino.

He returned home embittered. Is that how the Spanish regarded the Portuguese? How from the first hour we supported and participated in the struggle against the fascist uprising? Wasn't it a Portuguese officer instructing the Fifth Regiment in formation? Wasn't it an exiled Portuguese aviator who was one of the first to bomb rebel units? Didn't he just recently, here in Madrid with thousands of people, attend the funeral of a Portuguese combatant who fell heroically in the mountains at Guadarrama? Wasn't it a Portuguese who, along with the Durruti Column, headed and commanded one of the other columns that left Catalonia to advance into the interior occupied by the military rebels? And was it of no significance that he, and Manuel and Renato, were offering their solidarity—modest perhaps, but without doubt real and active? And as far as the International Brigades are concerned, didn't Gonzalo see that the Portuguese, integrated into Spanish social life, understanding the language and making themselves understood, were also joining Spanish units and—who knows?—would show up in the Brigades with Spanish names?

What did Tó Marcolino want? And maybe Gonzalo too? That the Portuguese, with their whole border occupied by the fascists on both sides, and on the Spanish side with deep war zones, should come swimming by the Atlantic Ocean?

Days later he came back to Renato to talk over what had happened. Now he had calmed down and was in a better mood. "What Tó Marcolino said is not the way so many, many *compañeros* we know and fight alongside think. Any old Tó Marcolino can say whatever he wants, but we will go on fulfilling our internationalist duty."

"Of course," Renato agreed.

3

Pepe was a live wire all right. He looked at everything, observed it all and commented freely. You could say he was just the opposite of Renato. Nevertheless, these two established a friendship. They worked their security shifts together and spent their free time together too, whenever there wasn't enough of it for Renato to return home. If it was daytime, they'd stroll along the avenues and imbibe a few draft beers. If it was night, Pepe left in a hurry without saying where he was headed, and Renato made himself comfortable in the courtyard sitting on a step of the stone staircase watching the mass of refugees crowding in.

One of those nights, when he was getting ready to take a nap, Pepe clapped him on the shoulder and made a signal not to say anything. "Come with me!"

Renato went. Pepe led him down a long corridor which gave access to the infirmary, sat down, told Renato to sit as well, opened up a newspaper and pretended to read.

"What's going on?" Renato asked.

"Shhhh," Pepe whispered.

After a few minutes, Pepe lightly squeezed Renato's arm to call his attention. At that moment, a man of a strange constitution was walking quickly down the corridor toward the exit. As the sweltering night descended upon the capital, it was hard to miss the suit jacket he was wearing and the cap perched on his head. He disappeared at the end of the corridor and Pepe stood suddenly, pulling Renato up to follow the man. "Come! Come!" he repeated.

Already outside the Socorro and on the sidewalk, Pepe looked quickly in both directions before choosing his direction. "This way!"

They stopped at a corner. "What's up?" Renato wanted to know.

"Don't you see him?" Pepe answered, pointing down the street.

Renato squinted to see, and finally noticed a figure crossing over to the other side up ahead. There was no doubt. It was the same guy who had run by them in the hospital corridor.

Renato went along with Pepe on the manhunt. When the man had passed them in the corridor, he had vaguely looked like Dr. Lorenzo, the young doctor who was renowned for trying to bed all the nurses. But why was Pepe going after him? Pepe himself was given to amorous adventures and hot pursuit.

Pepe pulled him brusquely into the well of a doorway where they kept still, observing.

The figure was standing, almost leaning on the front of a building, as immobile as they were. Did he sense he was being followed? He stood silently in the dark for some time. Then the figure took a couple of steps to the edge of the sidewalk, stood there, and returned to his former position.

Suddenly, another figure emerged from a cross street onto the same sidewalk. When he had approached a few meters, the man Pepe and Renato were pursuing moved in his direction, they joined up and continued down the street at a good pace.

The biggest surprise was the house to which they directed themselves, and which they entered, after stopping several times to verify that they weren't being followed. It was nothing more nor less than the Castellana, a small palace surrounded by a garden.

"Are we going?" Renato asked.

"We have to wait."

Renato remained for quite some time with his comrade waiting in ambush. Finally he came to a decision. "I'm leaving." And he left.

The next day, returning to the hospital for their security shift, Pepe said nothing about the incident and Renato didn't ask. They did their regular watchmen's rounds, and spent their free time together drinking beer, as though nothing had happened.

Until one day Renato, having seen Dr. Lorenzo as he normally would, had the sudden inspiration to ask the nurses about Tó Marcolino, whom he hadn't seen for a while.

"Tó Marcolino?" one of them said. "I don't know what happened, but he stopped coming to the hospital."

A few days later, Pepe exploded. "You're incredible! You haven't asked me anything about the man we were following."

"What of it?" Renato replied.

Pepe was shocked by Renato's lack of curiosity and put his cards on the table. He was serving there in the hospital security team, but that wasn't all. He was also with the special security service of the Republic, which was in the process of being organized. He knew Renato well and figured he could well be brought into their ranks.

"Don't even think about it," Renato grunted. "The police? Never! And the secret police? Even less!"

"I understand, *amigo*," Pepe said in a serious tone that was far from usual for him. "In Portugal, you got Salazar, the dictatorship, the State Defense Police, all repressing the people. Here—and now that we're at war—we're very short on our Republican police, our security for the Republic, and intelligence for the Republic. If we don't step up, they'll defeat us with a rearguard action."

As for the person they were chasing, he said in confidence, it was in fact Tó Marcolino. For a long time he'd been under watch. Finally they caught him—"

"Great," Renato interrupted. "I'm not interested in knowing any more—"

"Listen, *compañero*—"

"I'm not interested. That's your business, not mine."

They remained friends, as before, on watch, on guard, and on their free time. About this issue they never spoke again.

4

Few empty spaces could be seen throughout the vast old convent courtyard. Many were stretched out, others were sitting.

Some squeezed together in groups or covered themselves with light blankets. Others lay down right on the stone floor. Old people, women, children—it was a somber mountain of humanity, alive and suffering, though at first glance their stillness looked like death.

Seated on a step of the staircase during a break between assigned shifts, quietly and sadly watching the human multitude, Renato spotted two young boys quite near him closely embracing. The older one had a fixed, traumatized stare, the younger one was shy but observant. He approached them.

"Your mother?" he asked in a quiet voice. No response, and not even any movement.

"Your mother?" he repeated. "Your father?"

The only reaction was that the smaller boy closed in to even more tightly embrace the older boy in a gesture of defense and protection.

From under a blanket, a woman with a pallid face arose out of the reclining figures. "They don't talk...the boys—" she explained. "They were left that way."

Left? After what? Renato thought.

The woman continued. "The fascists killed their father, killed their mother, they killed their whole family—"

"Are you hungry" Renato asked.

The same fixed, shocked eyes stared back at him, and the watchful eyes of the younger. No response.

Someone tapped him on the shoulder. "They're calling for you." It was time to go back to work. He went, and never heard anything more about those two children.

From time to time Renato stopped back at his home. Isabel, his wife, insisted that he stay home and not subject himself to danger. He didn't lack the desire to stay, but then all that he had seen came back to mind. He reassured his wife that he wasn't facing any danger, that he was only putting in his shifts at the field hospital, not at the front. He always wound up staying home a little longer, until he got up and left, like someone calmly going to work.

He would have gone on with Pepe and the other workmates doing their security shifts if one day a stretcher bearer at the hospital hadn't been absent. That day had seen some big combat. With all the dead and wounded, teams needed to go to the front. Someone from the teams that had been called up to leave ran every which way trying to find the missing man. "Has anyone seen Juan Morales?" And again, "Has anyone seen Juan Morales?"

They passed by anxiously, once, twice, and from the street came the impatient, demanding ambulance siren.

A desperate cry filled the courtyard that they were missing one team member, and they needed someone, and could anyone offer to go?

The guy hadn't even finished making his appeal when a voice was heard. "I'll go."

It was Renato.

5

Where did the commanders come from if from the beginning there weren't any? In those first, decisive confrontations, who in the sierra had the talent to organize the popular forces, with no military training and poorly armed, to be able to cut off the fascist troops' advance—army units commanded by career officers with artillery, mortars and machine guns?

"*No pasarán!*" they shouted in Madrid. "They shall not pass!" And then they did not pass.

On the main roads that transversed the sierra, and in the few settlements, militias assumed positions equipped with light arms, and military faithful to the Republic with heavy arms.

On the mountains and slopes it was another situation.

As if guiding themselves by military maps which they did not have, thousands of civilians occupied the ridges and spread out over the hillsides to dominate the valleys and roads. Here and there they chose advantageous places to set up an ambush. When the enemy tried to move forward they were blocked by real moveable battles—attempts at encirclement, advances and retreats, the conquest and reconquest of positions. In various zones of the sierra temporary battle fields materialized, sometimes lasting hours and hours, where bodies were falling all over the place, targeted by the enemy owing to inadequate shelter or the flat terrain.

The stretcher bearers arrived under fire. Where bodies had fallen, that's where they ran, sometimes crawling, sometimes sprinting wildly, as if they could run faster than the bullets. At least it looked that way. How many times did Renato and his companions cross that same hillside under the most intense fire! How many times did they lift the wounded off the ground and bring them to a safer spot, exposing themselves to be newly targeted! How often, to stanch a hemorrhage, to quickly dress a wound, to tie a bandage, to apply a tourniquet, did they remain on the field without hurrying to get away or save themselves from that hell of pain and death! It's unknown, and impossible to know, how many times bullets missed them by centimeters, or even by millimeters, as though deviating from course to do justice and pay homage to a heroism that isn't spoken of so much as the heroism of those who fight with weapons in hand.

When he learned that Renato had gone to the front as a stretcher bearer and had conducted himself there with valor under fire to collect the wounded, António asked him, "Were you afraid?"

"Of what?" Renato answered.

António did not like that answer. *What bravado*, he thought. And at that moment his memory went back to the day he taught Renato to drive and the student, driving perfectly, told him he had never driven before. *What bravado*, he thought once again. Then he recalled the time they were at Guadarrama to resolve the matter of the boy accused of making signals to the enemy, and the nervousness he felt on the return trip when they crossed the road under bombardment.

"*Coño!*" he commented, inexplicably harshly. "Goddammit, no one can understand you."

And not quite knowing why, António also remembered that moment during the assault on Carabanchel when he and the others had stopped before fire from a nest of machine gunners, trying to silence the enemy, and he saw Manuel stand up, jump out of hiding, run under fire and—he only learned it was Manuel later on—attack the fascists from the rear, wiping out the resistance and opening the path to advance. Why? Why wasn't it he himself who did what Manuel did? Why did he not join him? What had happened to Manuel, and not happened to him, to lead them to such different postures? Such ruminations would not leave him, and he felt despondent with himself.

6

It was in such state of mind that, stopping by the Socorro, he got word that a Portuguese couple wanted to speak with him and had been waiting in the building since early morning.

He found them seated in a narrow corridor. They were a shocking sight, seated stiffly side by side, hands on their knees, as if they had been there forever. Their faces were frozen, rigid, with no change of expression. Their eyes were paralyzed, although possibly they still could see, and their mouths were void of affect. What a terrible apparition, what terrible faces! Underneath that deathlike rigor mortis, one could only guess at the intense anxiety of their interior life that had caused them to lose the capacity to express themselves.

What they wanted was very concrete: They wanted to find out something about their son Raul. He had left the house two weeks before, certainly to go off to war. They had no idea where he had gone nor where he was.

Even before the fascist coup, he had left the house and wandered the streets searching out places where the sharpest confrontations were occurring. What he did there, the parents did not know. Raul returned, but said nothing about where he had gone, nor what he had seen or done. It was dangerous in those days to walk around like that, still a child, only thirteen years old. He was risking a lot. He set them at ease whenever he came back to the house.

One day, though, the unease took on new proportions with the words uttered. "You're still a child, Raul. War is for grownups, not for you."

Raul answered angrily, "Why not for me?"

They tried to take his youth into account. But the incident at Guadarrama showed the situation was more serious. Raul went to the sierra with combatants and would have met a bad end had António and his friends not gone up there to save him from the unfair suspicion of making light signals to the enemy.

He had returned with their escort, and the father had admonished him. "I hope you learn your lesson, Raul. You could have ended up there," and he repeated what he had said before. "War is for grownups, not for children."

It was a mistake to underscore that point. Raul's answer came quickly and cruelly. "It's not for you, that's clear! You just like to sit at home smoking and listening to the radio."

A few days later he left and it was now several weeks since he had returned home. They couldn't wait any longer without trying to find him. They needed to know where he was, what happened to him, if he was alive or if he was dead. Their anxiety was unbearable.

What could António say to them? He said what he could. That he would try to find out if anyone had seen the boy. And that he'd ask the people at Guadarrama where he was, and if he had returned there. If he learned anything he'd let them know right away.

But how to sustain hope for any outcome in a such a world, so immense and so possessed by forces in movement and combat, with an infinite number of points of departure, ambition and chance, and a whole society in the furious throes of death and destruction? Not even he believed in the answer he gave them.

There is no feeling so grievous than that of losing sight of a beloved person and never knowing anything more about them—and not only not knowing, but admitting, at every turn with more reason to admit it, that you will never come to know. Never to know what happened, where he went, what he did. If he died, where and when. If he was alive—alive! alive! that endless and ever increasing yearning that it be true—where could he be and why doesn't he give a sign of life? Unknown soldiers, in this case a son, a child.

7

Still feeling moved by his encounter with Raul's parents, António was walking through a corridor at the hospital and almost bumped into a nurse with a white smock and cap standing before him. Dark and beautiful, she regarded him with a faint smile. She stood there waiting, without making room for him to pass.

The sudden recognition was a mixture of surprise and emotion.

"Celia! Here? That's fantastic!"

Yes, it was her, really her, the girl who stayed by him under the scalding sun in that wave of people in flight from the Badajoz area.

"You here, fantastic!" he said again.

"I'm happy to see you," Celia said, standing still and placidly looking at him.

So many things to ask, to know, to remember!

Just then a woman's voice called out with some urgency. "Celia!" Along with the call, another nurse gestured Celia to hurry up.

"It was a pleasure to see you. *Adiós!*" the young woman said simply. And turning around, she disappeared down the corridor, almost running.

He also hurried off to meetings that awaited him. His thoughts pursued him, though, from that unexpected reencounter—memories of unforgettable times, those days of tramping, pausing for rest, attraction, tenderness and generosity, and Celia's beautiful face framed by her headscarf, offering him bread and water. And now there in the hospital in her white uniform and the white cloth cap securing her hair, standing in front of him smiling and saying, "I'm happy to see you."

The next day he ran to the hospital. He looked up and down everywhere, when from the midst of a group of staff dressed in white smocks, the lovely, unmistakable brown face turned in his direction. She fixed her eyes on him, not smiling and waiting, like the day before, but just a glance with a hint of sadness, and then she looked away.

He went up to her. The woman turned to look at him, not with the smile he used to see, but rather with a surprising look of judgment and annoyance.

"Finally—" He was going to say more, but an arm extended out from the group and in a calm, natural, almost loving gesture, pulled Celia away. Paying no mind to António, that person brought Celia back into the group and gently led her away. The woman turned her head toward António for a brief second before the group went off.

Then António recognized who it was that had led her away, leaning in toward her and speaking to her surely in a soft voice: Dr. Lorenzo.

8

The first aerial bombardment took Madrid by surprise—brief, in peripheral zones, a warning. In the center deafening booms like cannon shots sounded. Only each one of them, separate from the others, lasted longer, its resonance lingering in the air. Later ambulance sirens screamed, and news reports arrived. More alarming than the bombardment itself was the fact that the planes were German. Thus the Hitler German intervention and military aggression were confirmed.

The populace set up shelters in basements and improvised services and alerts. That night the city went dark.

With this encouragement, the fascists came out of their lairs and launched new sorties and shootings. They calculated badly. The city was no longer in the first days of battle. Now there were armed forces and organized security units aside from the mass engagement of the population. Such attempts did not end well for their perpetrators, who were nabbed or shot down in the city streets.

The second bombardment was different. The alarm sirens went off. The old "firing range" at the field hospital turned into an immense infirmary. The refugees who filled the great entrance courtyard were led to the basement rooms. At that point a strange behavior occurred. The available staff did not remain in the cellars, nor did they go to reinforce the guards at the gate. They ran tripping up stairs and, searching the long corridors, found the route up to the roof. There they remained watching the sky.

With a droning roar, their red and green lights clearly visible, the three-engine Junkers Ju 52s flew over like veritable hurricanes in the sky. They came in at an apparently slow speed like gigantic black phantasms.

Booom!…Booooom!!…Boom!…Boooooom!!!

The track of rumbling thunder described the path of destruction and death they left in the city.

It was not just the horrific noise of motors and explosions that people heard. Tracing the same route as that of the enemy planes was the sound of brief pops, timid but in continuous bursts like firecrackers. Civilians went to the rooftops and fired their pistols at the passing planes, without even a hope of hitting their target. It was a protest, a declaration of determination and resistance.

Afterward, everyone descended into the streets. The ambulances and the stretcher bearers had already been dispatched. Renato and the others were clearing the ruins. By improvised light in the affected neighborhoods, they searched for the wounded and dead in the bombed-out buildings, gathered up the newly homeless, tried to contain the confusion, organized and directed the salvage work.

The bombardment was not aimed at any military targets. It was openly directed at urban districts, against the population at large, against Madrid—Madrid, capital of the Republic, Madrid of the people in arms—the Madrid that had smashed the revolt of an army equipped and commanded by the military hierarchy, Madrid that had halted the advance of Franco, who, with the help of Hitler, Mussolini and Salazar, had counted on a rapid victory.

The next day, at lunch time, António met Stockler when he went to a bar for a coffee. Stockler already had his opinion about the bombardments. "There's no cause for alarm," he pronounced. "It was a bad play on Hitler's part. He canceled out any rationale for nonintervention. England and France will intervene. They can't stay out of it now."

Isabel, Renato's wife, was manifestly not of the same opinion. The aerial bombardment only augmented her worry, and with good reason.

A few days after the bombardment, Renato was informed there was a woman outside looking for him. He went to see. It was Isabel. "I come to you begging," she said without elaboration. "Get me work so I can stay here."

That surprised Renato tremendously, but he proceeded as though it was something they had long agreed upon. Taking his wife's hand, he brought her to the hospital administration.

Gonzalo received them warmly, hired her into the cleaning service, and she didn't regret it. But if she was seeking greater tranquility, things worked out just the opposite. At home she could no longer stand being so far away, knowing that her husband was running considerable risk and her not knowing about it. Now the anxiousness was even more constant, punctuated by sharp blows of uncertainty. Every day, right in the hospital, there was news of departures for the front, and she was distraught with anticipation until she saw them return with the wounded. So her anxiety was much worse here. At home she would imagine the danger. Here she knew it, concretely, hour by hour.

Renato saw she was troubled. "Do you want to go back home?" he asked.

"How can you even ask that? No! Where you are, I will be."

9

One day not long afterward the ambulances and the back and forth of the stretcher bearers to the front were going non-stop.

"How many wounded today?" a doctor asked at Reception.

"Forty-eight."

"Less than yesterday."

"Yes, two less."

It was a question of statistics. Necessary statistics. Statistics at Reception in the field hospital. Statistics in the war communiqués. Statistics in the newspapers. How many? A number. A number also at the field hospital. There, however, not only a number. There, unspeakable human suffering. There, a panoramic portrait of the war.

You see war on the battlefield, in the horror of the bombardments, in the destructiveness, in the bodies that fall. But there is no place like a field hospital to intimately comprehend the actual meaning of human suffering that war creates, not in general, global, impersonal terms, but in concrete, individual stories.

You have to see that leg, split open, lacerated, the broken femur exposed, the giant bone sticking out from the flesh, skewered in blood. You have to see the wounded in all their horrendous variety, the cuts, the holes, the burns, so terrible and so final that, in many cases, with all the skills of the stretcher bearers, the doctors, the nurses, it's not so much the lives they're thinking about saving, but the pain they hope to mitigate, and human solidarity in an obligation to repair the evil that others have committed.

You have to hear the crying that brave men could not contain, and the groaning, the yelping, the panting, afflicted breathing, the throaty rattle of those on the verge of death.

You have to see that face, not just disfigured but crushed in a sea of blood and red clots, where nevertheless, despite all the ineffable pain, to our shock, we're conscious of that single eye that's fixed on us accusingly—to be sure not personally on us who see it, but on humanity, for its wars and crimes.

All this there, at Reception, in the improvised operating room, in the hospital wards, there, that day.

There, that day, forty-eight soldiers fallen at the front. Followed by another day, another week, another month, maybe another year of war. And the communiqués that coldly record the lists of statistics. In military terms, so many dead, so many wounded, so many unaccounted for. And at the end of the wars, statistics as cold as the crime itself: So many millions. More in this war than the last. It's history now. And the crime repeats itself.

So the days went. Every time Renato left for the front, his wife waited nervously for his return. She knew that every day he faced death innumerable times. Then when he returned, she felt such relief from the terrible weight of suspense. The situation repeated itself time after time, and time after time he returned alive. Unconsciously, Isabel had started feeling sure of his return.

Vain illusion. One day Renato departed for the sierra with the stretcher bearers and didn't come back. The team went back twice to look for him. Renato did not come in with the wounded, nor was he taken away with the dead. His *compañeros* had seen him fall, struck by bullets, but couldn't reach him because in the attack the fascists had occupied the terrain where he fell.

The next day at the hospital Renato's wife was seen wandering the halls looking quite lost. She continued her work cleaning the sick rooms, but from time to time she stopped work, disappeared to hide herself, certainly to have a good cry.

A few days later Isabel went to the hospital administration. She had a simple request: to be accepted onto the team of stretcher bearers. The request granted, she started going to the front every day. The last known reports made mention of her exceptional courage.

Chapter VII

1

STOCKLER for sure gave much thought to the aerial bombardment in the days afterward. Right away he came to some categorical conclusions. If Hitler intervened with aerial support, England and France would finally take a firm position. If necessary, they would send arms.

"What would you have?" he said to the Hotel Berne Group. "That England and France renounce their international responsibilities? They couldn't do that, and they won't do it."

The Hotel Berne people did not agree.

Dr. Melxior didn't enter the discussion. He had no intention of remaining in Spain, and was already getting his papers in order. His thought was to escape to Brazil. So he said confidentially to Stockler, who he figured would know a great deal about passports and safe-conducts having been a Portuguese consul.

Captain Roseiro came off evasively. Logically, that's how it should be, but he wasn't confident that it would. He predicted one thing and also its opposite. "You're right, Stockler. England and France can't stand by without taking a firm position. They most certainly will. But you know the power Hitler has. It would be craziness to pursue such adventures and risk making a wrong move. For that reason it's almost certain they will hold out and wait."

"You're wrong, Captain!" Stockler replied. "If Germany intervenes, they'll intervene too."

Not much time had to pass before the facts disproved this prediction. The Junkers came back with more bombardments, and there was talk of Italian troops ready to intervene, but not a word came out of England, and from the Socialist Léon Blum, Prime Minister of France, came a flurry of pretentious words, but as for the concrete support needed, nothing. And no arms. In the face of such realities, Stockler changed his opinion a hundred and eighty degrees—contradictorily, at the precise moment when Madrid received and celebrated in the streets the arrival of new weapons. Forces from the Fifth Regiment paraded with rifles at their shoulders—hundreds of rifles with butts of yellow wood. Finally the necessary help came, from the other side of the Atlantic, from Mexico. But it came. As they marched by, people applauded from the sidewalks.

"There's no doubt about it," Stockler confessed, "I was wrong. England and France are on their knees. And now? If they don't intervene, how are the Spanish people going to resist? With Mexican rifles? The butts are very pretty, very cheery. But is the Spanish Republic going to go up against Hitler's planes and Mussolini's troops with rifles?"

From that day forward, the two started meeting more often, Stockler and the doctor. Their trips to the Embassy of Brazil became an almost daily event, seeking to obtain political asylum and the paperwork required to go there.

2

With the international picture looking as it did, the question insinuated itself persistently. How did people truly see the outcome of the war? A fascist defeat? The victory of the

Republic and the people's revolution in response to the coup? Or the military crushing of the Republic, the predictable general massacre and the installation of a bloody Franco dictatorship? Who could assess the reality most clearly? Those who were rushing to try and get to Brazil, or those who every day proclaimed, "We will win the war!"

António needed to exchange views about all this with someone. But with whom? Among the Portuguese, maybe only Manuel, but when they'd have the chance, he didn't know. And with whom among the Spaniards? Gonzalo had no time for anything. At the Central Committee of the PCE António's meetings were always rushed and only to attend to business. Eulalia? But who could say when he'd find her? The opportunity arose, however, unexpectedly.

One day he ran into Rubio, who had come to Madrid from the Toledo front on a special mission. They conversed at some length, and António finally posed the question. "What do you think, Rubio? Are we going to win the war? Or lose it?"

"We're fighting to win it," Rubio responded.

"We're fighting to win it, very well. But what do you really think? Not just what we want but what can we foresee?" He, António, couldn't close his eyes to the reality that Stockler was ultimately pointing—

"That guy is a coward," Rubio interrupted. "The only thing he wants to save is his own skin."

Even if he is a coward, even if he just wants to save his own skin, that's not the question, António insisted. The question was if, with the international situation as it stood, the Spanish people had sufficient forces to defeat Franco's troops and intervention by Germany, Italy, and Salazar. "I have my doubts, Rubio. I'm just saying this to you, and only to you. I have them, why should I deny it to myself?"

"Then I'm going to remove them from you," Rubio said. And he ticked off his contrary arguments.

First, the will and the heroism of the Spanish people. Then that the Spanish people were not alone in the world. The Soviet Union supported the struggle for the Spanish Republic and wouldn't abandon it. And then there was the solidarity from Communists and workers and democratic forces throughout the world. Just now, comrades from Germany, Bulgaria, Italy were arriving, and the International Brigades were in formation. So there were still many trump cards to play.

"Will it be enough?" António needed to know.

It seemed as though everything had been said. But it wasn't. Rubio started talking further, slowly measuring his words, not his usual manner.

"The facts you cite are real facts. I'm constantly reminded of them myself. They are objective givens of the situation."

"You don't want to say you have doubts, but neither are you saying you're certain of victory."

"Certain is a terrible word," Rubio said. "If people seeking to guarantee their rights fight only when they are certain of victory, they would never have fought. Freedom, social rights, the October socialist revolution, the great victorious struggles of the workers and oppressed peoples, all were possible because workers and the peoples in every case fought for victory with confidence—but not with certainty that they'd succeed."

"Then how is confidence possible?" António continued probing.

"Confidence is not being certain. I remember what a *compañero* told me a few days ago: If you only fight for what you're sure of, and if what is actually happening is the only sure thing, that's the same as not doing anything—giving up the struggle and accepting eternal submission to exploitation, oppression and injustice. The fascists have declared war on our people. We have to fight, and fight not with the idea that it's a losing cause, but to win."

After another pause, Rubio added, "I love life. But if I have to choose between life and death, then, as La Pasionaria says, 'It's better to die on your feet than to live on your knees.'"

3

António felt a great sense of trust—of confidence—in Rubio, and it was good for António to hear him out. But what did he know of Rubio? In the end, very little. He had gotten to know him in the column that was blasted apart on the way to Badajoz. He met him again, a survivor like himself, on the truck returning to Madrid. He had gone with him to try out weapons at the "firing range" and together were amused by the scene where the Smith 32 flubbed with a broken firing pin. Later, Rubio took António's Lancia, leaving him that humorous, friendly letter. Rubio came and went, simple, straightforward, and happy. That's what António knew of him. He never asked if Rubio had participated in combat, in which combats and how he had fought. Rubio also didn't volunteer anything about himself. Obviously it was a long story. But António came to learn something of it without Rubio's ever having said anything.

He went to the usual place at the Socorro where he had his meetings. He had just finished speaking with Rubio when Gonzalo, who had seen them together, asked, ""Do you know Rubio well?"

"Yes, I know him very well."

"Do you know what he is now?"

"What he is? Yes, I know, he's going back to the front one more time."

"You don't know anything else?"

"Like what? What are you trying to say?"

"Like, Rubio has become a true commander on the front. The Government has just established the Mixed Brigades of the People's Army. It's about reorganizing and radically reinforcing our armed forces. Rubio has just been named political commissar of one of those brigades."

That news generated a confused mixture of shock, satisfaction and melancholy.

"Wow, magnificent!" António didn't know what else to say.

The next day by chance he found Rubio once again. He didn't indicate that he knew anything, and didn't ask anything. Rubio, as always needing a shave, with his blond hair rigid as wire, his blue eyes looking directly at António, was the first to speak—as if he had not had the conversation the day before.

"You can rest assured, I'm not taking your car tomorrow—"

António did not give any sign of knowing what Gonzalo had told him. "And if you did? I'd go requisition another!"

"Requisition?" They both knew that requisitioning anything saying "*uachepé*" had ended quite some time ago.

And both of them felt the pleasure in recalling the course of their meeting and friendship, their frank, spontaneous camaraderie, with its own natural rhythms of expanding and deepening their mutual understanding. As comrades, combatants, friends and human beings.

4

For reasons other than those of Stockler and the Captain, The Comrade was also considering leaving Spain. He brought António up to date on his decision. The war was going to endure. The fascists occupied the entire border, and to get there from any direction they'd have to go through a war zone. He could not return to Portugal overland. "We can't go by foot," he summarized ironically.

He had already spoken with the Spanish comrades now in the government of Largo Caballero. They could help. He would try to enter France, via Catalonia, and from France to Portugal by ship. Clandestinely, of course. "There are cargo ships going to Portugal. They have holds and whaleboats. We have friends among the sailors and fishermen. It wouldn't be the first time."

António's responsibility for border crossings now no longer made sense. But he should remain in Madrid. It was still necessary to have someone the Party could always go to, who would maintain contact with the Spanish comrades, to help provide secure housing to some comrade who might arrive later.

António reacted. "You mean, stay here with nothing to do!"

The Comrade explained that what he was proposing was highly important. If it wasn't António, who would it be? Besides which, there was a lot to do in Madrid. Cultivate the ties with émigré Portuguese democratic forces, give support in the capital to the Portuguese combatants and others who might turn up. To António these all seemed like a pile-up of arguments, but not real reasons.

"It's a very uncomfortable situation you're proposing for me. The others are out there fighting, risking their lives, and I'm here peacefully in the rearguard. No, I'm not at all pleased with this arrangement."

The Comrade insisted. "The interests of the Party require—"
"The interests of the Party," António repeated, with an irritation he rarely displayed. "And the wishes of the militants don't count?"
The Comrade emphatically did not understand such a reaction. Couldn't António say what he needed to say without getting excited, and talk to him with a cool head? Couldn't they better resolve the issues before them together? Or was António opposing his opinion, not so much to that of The Comrade, but to himself?

5

Having spoken with António, The Comrade wished to speak with Manuel. António informed him that it had been quite some time since he had come to Madrid. As soon as he came, António would tell him to go see The Comrade. That's the way they left it.
Manuel appeared at the house, and Madrecita embraced him hungrily. "Manolo, *hijo mío*. How you've made me suffer! The days go by and I know you're at the front, and I don't hear any news of you—" She paused briefly. "The same with Eulalia. I have no idea where she is—surely risking her life. And I don't know anything. Nothing, nothing!"
António told Manuel what The Comrade had proposed to him and the reasons he was unhappy with it. It wasn't right that he remain there, knowing the others were out risking their lives at the front, and him meeting a few people on the esplanades and waiting for someone to appear. "I find it impossible to accept a situation like that."
Manuel tried to convince him otherwise. He said The Comrade was right, and that the need did exist for someone trustworthy to remain in Madrid to take care of those kinds of tasks.
"No, no, and no!" And they ended the discussion without agreement.
As he had said to António, The Comrade told Manuel he was returning to Portugal and that he shouldn't wait any longer. He had come on a mission, and had discharged part of it. The other part of the mission he could not accomplish, because the

prison in Huelva, where two comrades in the leadership were being held, had fallen into fascist hands right after the coup started. Nothing could be done to free them—if they hadn't been killed already. Now it was time to go back. The war in Spain posed new tasks in Portugal, and the cadres in the Party were few.

The Comrade had been thinking. Even in Portugal he had heard much about Manuel as a militant youth leader. He knew about the agitation incident at the Public Fair. He saw the courage Manuel exhibited as a combatant.

"My idea is very clear," he concluded. "If you wish to go to Portugal with me, I'll settle everything and you can leave with me now. I take responsibility for the decision. The comrades will understand and be pleased."

Manuel hesitated to respond. A whirlwind of tangled and contradictory thoughts, ideas and memories evoked feelings both of satisfaction and of bitterness and uncertainty. The confidence The Comrade showed in him, the desire to continue the struggle inside the country—which had been his own wish at the time it was decided that he emigrate—the vision of being once again in his company of young Communists, his *companheiros* of so many struggles, these and so many other things came to mind, not to mention the fond memory of Lisbon and its unparalleled atmosphere, the contented houses on the hills, the river, the sun, the ocean.

And then the road he had traveled since Franco's coup, all that was different and big in his life, in the streets of Madrid and at Carabanchel with António, and then at Guadarrama and Somosierra, with Pablo and Alonso, with Jaime and Consuelo, with others, making a common front against the fascist assault, sometimes saving people's lives even as he placed his own in danger, other times saving his own because his *compañeros* on their part were risking their own. And more. Out of the dizzying swell of thoughts came the unanticipated recollection of Eulalia, his great friend smiling with the charm of that one twisted tooth....

"I'm staying."

He explained in brief words. Yes, he would like very much to return to Portugal and resume the struggle there. But now he was here, with the Spanish people, with his companions risking their blood. He had such a bright living memory of Consuelo, so young, so slender and lithe, audacious beyond limits, braver than any of the others and, alas, one of the first to fall into the earth like a bloody ragamuffin.

"Where she died, at my side, I will continue with the other comrades. I feel that's best for me."

6

The Comrade worked things out and departed.

Within days, Gonzalo called António to his office. "This is to inform you there are problems with your *compañero* in Catalonia. They're not allowing him to continue his journey."

After another week António received a letter from Barcelona. The party hadn't counted on the situation there, and it was best if António knew about it for his ongoing work and in planning other trips to that region.

The Comrade had received two documents from the PCE—a passport as a Spanish citizen and a party credential saying the bearer was traveling to France on a special mission.

According to the directions he had received, he had presented himself at the headquarters of the Partit Socialista Unificat de Catalunya (PSUC), the PCE's allied party in Catalonia, to ask them for help securing the necessary visa so he could leave the country. He was then directed to the anarchist command, the politico-military authority of Catalonia at that time.

"We will not permit this," they immediately responded when he presented the passport. "Who gave you this passport? Your place is in the militias, and we won't let you escape to France. Go back to Madrid and do your duty." Having said which, they paid him no further consideration.

The Comrade went back to the PSUC and told them what happened. "Go back there and present them the PCE credential and also this other one from our party attesting to the first one. They'll give you the visa now."

He went, but nothing worked there.

"Communist?! Two credentials! Who's your sponsor? Special mission to France? What special mission?"

"That's a party matter. I'm not at liberty to say."

"That's what you say. Without knowing what you're going to do we won't give you the visa."

"You have to understand the situation," they told him at the PSUC. "The anarchists have absolute power here. We can't do any more for you. Return to Madrid and the comrades there will think of something."

But The Comrade was not going to give up. He thought it through and a bizarre idea came to him, so bizarre that as it occurred to him, it seemed like utter foolishness. Then he took it to heart and went again to the anarchist command.

He asked for the same person who had attended him before, saying he needed to speak with him, but only with him, without anyone else listening.

In a private conference room he lowered his voice and explained his "mission." There was a ship anchored in Genoa loaded with arms for Franco, ready to sail out in a matter of days. The Comrade's mission was to go to Italy and sabotage the ship. Everything was set for him to receive the necessary assistance in France and in Italy.

The story came out of him just like that. Later he had to admit to himself how easy it was to lie, almost believing what he was saying. "I'm just telling this to you, *compañero*," he added. "I trust you won't say anything to anybody. My party would never forgive me—"

"You can be sure," the anarchist confirmed. He said to wait a bit, he left the room and came back shortly.

"Here you go." On a narrow table he stamped the visa in the passport. As he handed it to him he asked, "Do you have any Spanish money?"

"Yes, I do."

"You can't take it into France. At the border, leave it in the strongbox of the CNT, the Confederación Nacional del Trabajo."

"Of course!" and he wondered why the anarchist comrade actually believed his response.

And so he managed to cross into France, on his way to Portugal.

In the letter to António, and in another that he wrote to the PCE, The Comrade didn't relate the whole story. He just gave the essentials, which was all that mattered.

"That's how the anarchists are," Gonzalo told António. "Here in Madrid they repudiate the authority of the government and do whatever the hell they want. But now in Catalonia they exercise absolute power."

7

Manuel decided to stay. He felt better for it, remaining with thousands of other combatants. The people's army was gathering strength. International solidarity was growing. Military commanders and political commissars were born of the people's armed struggle.

The progression of the fascist advance was now blocked not solely and fundamentally by the people in arms, but also by the Republican Army which rapidly took shape.

And then, according to the comrades, with the formation of Largo Caballero's government, all the vacillation came to an end. "Finally it's the government of the Popular Front," Madrecita said. "Our *compañeros* are now in the government. The fascists will notice the difference."

For Madrecita too it was cause for fresh hope. What did António think? With comrades in the government would the war end sooner?

"I hope so," António said, adding no more.

He also believed that the entrance of Communists into the government would be decisive in organizing, disciplining and unifying the armed forces of the Republic, but he didn't feel so optimistic that the results would show right away.

Franco set up his general headquarters in Seville. Rumor had it that, proclaiming himself Chief of State and Generalísimo, he would install himself in Burgos as the capital. In the north, Irún fell. On the road to Madrid, Talavera de la Reina and Toledo had also fallen. The fascists turned up at the different fronts each time with ever more powerful weapons. The German and Italian intervention intensified.

In such a complex situation, António reflected for long hours after the reactions he got conversing with The Comrade and Manuel. Over and over he ruminated on what each one had told him. He felt strange conceding to stay in Madrid having his little talks and meetings and waiting for someone to appear while the war was devastating the whole of Spain and his comrades were risking their lives on the front lines. At the same time he knew that the tasks assigned to him were important; in fact, he better understood their importance when he imagined the grave situations that would arise if no one took charge of these functions. After a great deal of thinking he wound up concluding that at the end of the day it was the party that had framed the question and he, as a party member, should not refuse. Having arrived at that conclusion, he started to act.

He asked to be assigned an office at the Socorro where he could keep his papers, work, receive *compañeros* and conduct small meetings. He asked for a typewriter and ribbon, paper and carbon paper. He asked for a place where, apart from Eulalia's house, he could eventually spend the night. In the next few days, once he had made his requests, he realized it was hard to limit himself to that. What more could he do? Come to the office, see if there was anything he needed to do, read the papers or listen to the radio? Seek out the Hotel Berne people at a café or esplanade and hang around to chat? Go back to the house and confirm that everything was ready to receive comrades? Talk more with this guy, or more with that democrat, and exchange ideas about the eventual formation of a Portuguese Popular Front that right now didn't look like it would have many participating groups?

Amidst this monotonous routine, what certainly sustained him were the welcome from Madrecita and the visits with Fernando Torres. There he was at home with friends, the conversation was productive, he learned things, and his inner dissatisfaction calmed down a little.

He seemed just about convinced that his decision was right to continue with such tasks, when a small incident once again made him confused.

It was a casual encounter with Pepe, who had been Renato's *compañero* on the Gran Vía and later on guard watch in the building.

"So you've stayed here?" Pepe asked him. "We lost Renato," he added. "He died at the front. He wasn't the kind of man to stay behind in the rear guard. He was a brave one."

Was Pepe insinuating something? A criticism? An insult? Or was he merely, with no other intent, fondly remembering his companion and friend?

8

"Antón, *hijo mío*, what's wrong?" Madrecita asked when he returned to the house that afternoon. "Always in such a good mood and now so quiet and sad? What's wrong?"
"Nothing, Madrecita. Everything's all right."
But no, everything was not all right. In truth, he did feel sad. He couldn't rid Pepe's words out of his brain.
He went out in the morning with no destination in mind. He found himself in front of the automobile repair shop where he had worked, now long closed. Inside, thrown to one side, was his motorcycle that never got repaired. His very own cycle, on which he happily launched into acrobatic displays, his hands gripping the handlebars, legs up in the air, right there on the little streets behind the Socorro, to the admiration and applause of the young folks who gathered to see him. That crazy ride with Renato driving around the curves of the Guadarrama road also came to mind, with Barata in the back seat screaming with fear and Renato and himself mocking him. Remembering and thinking, he strolled down the Gran Vía that had been so badly punished by fascist terrorism, he walked through the narrow streets of the old city, seeing the esplanades and the cafés as he passed where he had met up with his comrades so many times. Suddenly, he couldn't say why, the idea came to him of stopping by the house of Raul's parents.
Several weeks had passed since they had come looking for him at the hospital in desperation. Maybe in the meantime the boy had come back home. Otherwise, though he could not bring the good news they were hoping to receive, perhaps he could still be useful, helping them with something else.
Despite numerous efforts, he had not obtained any news of the boy. Etched into his memory were the frozen faces of the father and mother the last time he had seen them. What could he tell them? When he arrived, he told them he had no news of their son, but he had come to see if they needed anything.

The response came slowly. The father who had been speechless and immobile, remained speechless and immobile. The only thing they needed, António couldn't give them. They didn't ask for anything, nor say anything. As he said goodbye, they still had no words. It was only at the very last moment that the wife, as if trying to explain the situation, pointed to her husband. "Poor thing. He doesn't even listen to the radio anymore."

Day by day, the fighting got more and more intense. The fascists had conquered Talavera, but had not yet been able to break their way through to Madrid. Their offensives continued to be contained at Guadarrama, Somosierra and other fronts where the Republicans concentrated their forces. António saw the incessant rotation of ambulances and stretcher bearers. Statistics came in of more dead and wounded. There was no sign of Manuel, nor did he return to the house. Every day, the comings and goings of the stretcher bearers brought to mind countless times the memory of Renato and his words when he was asked if he was afraid under fire. "Of what?"

Now it was Isabel, Renato's widow, who went out with the stretcher bearers. Though pale and thin, she demonstrated great energy.

For some obscure, unknown reason, when he met her at the hospital António put the same question to her that he had asked of her husband: "When you're out there, aren't you afraid?"

Maybe he expected the same extraordinary response Renato gave him, "Of what?"

She shrugged her shoulders and also pronounced two words, slightly different but the same. "So what?"

Chapter VIII

1

SEVERAL days later two nurses passed António and he heard one of them say to the other, "The sulfamide is for the Portuguese guy."

Portuguese? He ran after them. "Excuse me, Miss, what did you say about a Portuguese?"

"Nothing, he's one of the wounded."

"Here in the hospital? A Portuguese?"

"Yes, why?"

"'Cause that's what I am too." He asked that they show him his bed and he went to see him.

Lying on his back, his head and face wrapped in bandages, he had a long dressing covering one ear. The face was a raw wreck, swollen and minced with lesions. He seemed to be passed out. António was about to ask who the wounded man was when, fixing his gaze on the uncovered half of the face, it struck him: It was Manuel.

The doctors told him that the wounds were extensive but not very serious—a scrape on the scalp, a long but superficial slash across one cheek, and a bullet in the arm but no fracture. He had already been there two weeks. In another two weeks, three max, he'd be released.

António could hardly believe it—Manuel lying there for more than two weeks, and António going to the building every day never knowing he was there nor how and when he'd been wounded.

He would find out later. Not from Manuel who, unlike many others, didn't brag about his feats. Others told him.

It was on the same exact day of the big battle when Renato was up in the sierra and disappeared. That place came to be known as Somosierra.

On the hillside, the first-line positions had remained solid for a long time with no change. The distance separating the two enemy forces was but a hundred meters or so, with no trenches, no bunkers, no barricades. The only places of shelter were the dips in the terrain, boulders, tufts of foliage reinforced by improvised trenches or barricades.

The fascists had better material means, namely mortars and machine guns. The Republicans, aside from their courage and their own combat method, had acquired the advantage in positioning—principally, on a natural ledge, with a black boulder of a weird shape that made defense easier and allowed them, owing to the layout of the land, to forge out in counterattack when the enemy tried to advance.

In Somosierra people spoke about that black rock cliff and the repeated, violent fascist attacks to break through there, and about the successful Republican defense.

That day, once more, Manuel and his companions fought with their usual courage.

At Somosierra it was widely admired how the already well-known Consuelo Núñez Brigade, a unit of young combatants now reinforced by many others, had managed to resist for weeks on end. And how for two days and two nights they held back a violent attack—the fascists had machine guns, mortars and grenades. Two days and two nights! The brigade's special way of fighting had become famous, always by small but clever advance moves. Mobile and quick, they flitted over the terrain, changing positions, disorienting the enemy, surprising them with fire where they least expected it. They became notable, above all, for the audacity of their sneak incursions attacking the enemy at their rear.

On that day Manuel was wounded, and Jaime killed.

Now António stood before his comrade, passed out and almost unrecognizable. Fortunately the wounds were not as bad as they looked. After a few more days Manuel could talk, and António went back to visit him often.

António let the others know, and Madrecita went to visit, bringing a package of *churros* and carrying on jovially. "You're alive, son, that's what counts. This business with your face will clear up and you'll come back handsome as ever."

"Eulalia?" Manuel asked.

A month earlier, she had left Madrid on a mission, but Madrecita didn't know what. She suspected it would be risky and dangerous, but that's not how her daughter had put it. She reappeared a few days ago, but then left shortly, and hadn't come back yet. "What a shame!" she changed subjects. "If she had known you were here in the hospital, for sure she would have come to see you—"

"And her health?" She was okay, and Madrecita didn't say more.

Certainly there was more to be told that would have been of interest for Manuel to know. With an uncharacteristic reserve, Madrecita didn't add anything further.

At that moment the staff brought more of the wounded into the hospital ward and asked the visitors to leave.

The paucity of news gave Manuel new cause for anxiousness—indefinable, fleeting and recurring.

2

On one of his visits, António raised the subject and went directly to it. He hadn't spoken to anyone about what was on his mind. It's only with Manuel that he wanted to talk. The comrades had decided that he stay in Madrid, and had assigned him certain tasks. He'd thought about it a lot, and it seemed to him that decision had been made not because of the importance of the tasks, but because they had concluded he was afraid of war. And the worst of it was that he concluded they were right. "Yes, I am afraid of war."

Manuel, usually so even-tempered, interrupted him. "You're nuts."

"No, I'm not nuts."

And as it looked like Manuel was about to interrupt him again, he spoke louder. "Let me talk, because I need to talk. Do you remember what happened at the gate at the Cuartel de la Montaña? You went in, and I stayed out. Remember Carabanchel? You advanced and I stayed behind. You are brave—"

Manuel again tried to interrupt him, but António went on. "No, let me speak. You are brave. I'm not."

Manuel objected. Where did he get these ideas? What was wrong with him? They advanced together at the assault at the Cuartel, and they'd fought side by side in the attack at Carabanchel. So he, Manuel, may have run more, but that's all.

No, that was not all, and it wasn't only that. Look at Renato. António believed Renato had decided to remain protected on the rear guard, but he became a stretcher bearer and went to the front every day, to the areas of the greatest danger, and when António had asked if he was afraid, Manuel, can you imagine what he answered. He answered, "Of what?" Yes, Renato was a brave man. And he fell like a hero.

"I need to prove to myself that I'm not a coward."

"You aren't."

"I don't know if I am or not, Manuel. I haven't really had the chance to prove myself."

3

The chance to prove himself. If not yet a decision, it was an idea that wouldn't go away.

One time, coming back to the house, he exchanged a few hurried words with Madrecita, then said he needed to arrange a few things and went into his room.

Madrecita did not sleep peacefully. She found António agitated and sad. For hours and hours, she saw the strip of light coming from under his door while she heard him moving things around.

Finally the light from his room went off. With her sensitive hearing, Madrecita didn't get to sleep. By the sounds coming from his room, by unusual noises that broke the silence from time to time, she deduced that António also wasn't sleeping.

She was not mistaken. He wasn't sleeping. Many reassuring memories flooded his brain. These few weeks since Franco's coup had been the most dangerous of his life, the most frantic and upsetting. They had drawn responses out of him that he never imagined he had in him. And what he saw in himself, he also saw happening with other people. He never suspected, not even dreamed what he recognized now not only in others but in himself, that there existed within the human being such potential to soar far beyond what any individual had believed possible. Manuel, Renato, Isabel, Rubio, Eulalia, Madrecita, Raul and others, one after another, all passed through his mind. After so many weeks of dissatisfaction, questioning, doubting and anguish, these hours of insomnia came to him almost as a gift of reflection and peace.

Into this unspooling coil of memories and feelings the exchange of words he had had one time with Manuel also came to mind. When António was outraged by the case of the hospital director Tó Marcolino, he had said, "The truth is, Manuel, there are a lot of evil people in this world."

He remembered now what Manuel had answered. "The extraordinary thing, António, is how many good people there are in the world."

With those thoughts he finally got to sleep. It was already dawning. Who did not get to sleep was Madrecita. António got up early and Madrecita was already up and about. "Don't you want breakfast, Antón?"

No, he'd eat in town.

"Antón, *hijo mío*, what's wrong? You look so sad."

"No, Madrecita, I'm not any more, I assure you," and he gave her a kiss.

"When are you coming back?"

"Maybe tomorrow or the day after, at night."

"Come back soon. I want to see you."

4

When he arrived at the Socorro, Abel was already there. He had come to fetch António for a meeting with his father, Fernando Torres, who had a pressing need to speak with him.

They got in the car and talked along the way. "What are you up to now, *amigo*?"

"I'm looking at things and I study."

António knew that his father had been thinking about sending the boy to France or England. Had they decided yet? he asked. No, they decided not to. They weren't rich, you know. They were waiting for the war to end. And then, even if his parents stayed abroad, he would return to Portugal and continue his studies.

"And in the meantime you're staying here?"

"Yes, definitely. I'm learning a lot."

Then António directly approached the question. He'd been thinking about this overnight. The boy had the capacity, and what António wanted to propose lay within his reach. Did he want to assume some responsibility? Easy, but important. It involved going regularly to the Socorro and the party office. If a party leader showed up, Abel would take them to a house where they would stay. If other Portuguese arrived, he'd see what they needed and coordinate it with the Spaniards.

"That's all?"

"That, and little more."

"I accept. I'll tell my dad, is that okay?"

When they got to the house, Abel took his father aside and let him know he had accepted the proposed assignment.

Fernando Torres took this notice naturally as a decided thing. His face was at ease, and he appeared unmoved. Abel, who knew him well, understood that although with uncertainty, he liked the news.

He only said, "Don't take too many risks."

The next day, António brought Abel to Eulalia's house. Madrecita hugged António gladly, and Abel with reserve. "Antón, Antón, are you bringing a child into the war? He's of an age to live, not to die."

António explained it wasn't about that, and Madrecita felt much relieved.

5

Manuel was not expecting what António came to say on his next visit to the infirmary. He sat on the edge of Manuel's bed and didn't waste time. "I came to tell you I won't be staying in Madrid."

What? Manuel thought. In their last conversation he had said he understood where his duty lay and he had to stay because that was in the best interest of the Party. "But you yourself said just a few days ago that you understood and accepted—"

"No, I'm not staying. I'm not, and it's decided."

It didn't seem right to Manuel. The last time António told him he'd made a decision, and now he shows up with the opposite decision. Manuel didn't get it. "Why didn't you come see me? We've always talked everything over. Why did you keep your thinking from me?"

He paused briefly. "You come here all of a sudden and tell me 'I'm not staying after all.' Didn't you trust whatever opinions I might offer you? Were you afraid I'd convince you otherwise?"

After so many frustrating weeks, António displayed a surprising calm. "No, *amigo*. It wasn't about not trusting your opinion. To the contrary, it's because I do trust it. I already knew what you would tell me, and no, I didn't want you to convince me."

"You won't do this," Manuel underscored his point.

"I will. It's decided. I will."

The conversation stopped for a bit. António appeared to be reflecting further, then added, "I've already made arrangements. Everything is set with the *compañeros*. I'm going out with a unit of the Fifth Regiment. To the Aragón front."

"You won't do this—"

"I will. Later tonight I'm meeting with the comrades to see when we depart." After another brief pause, he hesitantly revealed the secret. "We're leaving tomorrow."

What else could Manuel say? "All right then. Let's talk about something else." And he asked if Eulalia had come to the house and if he knew anything about her. No, there was no news from her.

A nurse came in to say it was late and António had to leave.

They shook hands, their grasp lingering many seconds. António leaned over his friend and gave him a careful *abrazo*.
"Look for me when you get back," Manuel said.
"Certainly," António answered.

6

Manuel was released from the hospital on schedule. He had a long reddish scar from one ear all the way up to the top of his scalp, a smear of mercurochrome across his eyebrow, and his arm swinging freely but still bandaged. He had to return to the hospital two or three more times for check-ups.

Madrecita greeted him with effusive enthusiasm. "Finally you're home again, *hijo mío*. You'll get better here."

"Eulalia?"

No, she hadn't come back. In the absence of news, she couldn't sleep. "And you, Manolo? You're staying to get well, right?"

"Yes," Manuel agreed.

The conversation then took another turn. "Tell me something," Madrecita asked, "what's happening with António? He brought a lovely young boy here to take his place. What's going on?"

"Nothing special, Madrecita. War is war. They assigned him to another mission."

"Dangerous? Tell me the truth."

"Certainly, *compañera*. In war all missions are dangerous."

"Tell me, Manolo. Did António go the front too?"

"I don't know, Madrecita."

She didn't ask any more questions. Maybe she believed him, maybe not. She went to the kitchen and brought a basket of fruit to the dining room table, with a plate and knife.

"You know, Manolo. Eulalia's partner was assassinated. I've had no word of her. I don't know where she is nor what's become of her. Renato died. You're at the front, and every day I'm hoping you're alive. Now Antón is gone. You know, *hijo*, I do know war is war—but I wouldn't want to lose you all."

They continued talking for a good while longer. "Forgive me, *hijo*, for talking so much. You've just come from the hospital, you're hurt and you need to rest. Go lie down now, go."

So the days passed, Madrecita doing everything possible as a caregiver. Manuel returned to the hospital for his last appointments and treatment. He got up late, got dressed, listened to the news on the radio. He obeyed his medical instructions. But his impatience started to show. He felt the urge to go back to the front, to know what was happening there. To know about Alonso, Pablo and the other *compañeros*. All this time, Eulalia hadn't appeared, and it pained him to leave without knowing anything more about her.

"I'm leaving tomorrow," he announced.

"Manolo, Manolo, the war's not ending tomorrow. You still have plenty of time to go the front. Besides, Eulalia will come and will be very sad not to see you."

7

At Somosierra, Manuel joined up with the brigade in the heat of combat. A young militiaman he didn't know showed him his place alongside two others that he didn't know either. Why wasn't he put with Pablo? Why not with Alonso? Could they have fallen too, like Consuelo, like Jaime?

The objective was to prevent the enemy advance, with a barrier of grapeshot in places where the enemy would try to pass. From the other side a hailstorm of bullets picked at the protective boulders and earthen bags trying to silence the defense, but it failed. One of the enemy who dared an audacious sortie over uncovered terrain fell as soon as he had been spotted. Others, crawling over the ground, had trouble recovering the wounded man.

The confrontation didn't last long. The gunfire stopped and members of the brigade could reinforce their positions.

No one seemed to notice the highly visible record of the wounds on Manuel's face. He was alive and back at the front lines. Signs of far more serious wounds could be seen every day.

Alonso and Pablo were there, unharmed and confident as ever. "See, Manuel? No one can defeat us."

So it seemed, in fact, because as time passed, the fascists could not succeed in breaking through there. "Those guys are exhausted and used up."

The very next day, such words were no longer true. The fascists returned to the attack now reinforced with mortars. "We have to get out and catch them where they don't expect us," Manuel proposed.

With everyone agreed, and taking up once again the special tactics of the brigade, he, Pablo and three other young fellows retreated up into the sierra, clambering over hillsides, scaling cliffs and seeking out a path downward, presumably an impassable one. There they were, ensconced off to one side and above the line of the enemy mortars.

They didn't count on the fact that the fascists had prepared, and imagined and done the same. When the defenders were set to open fire and attack, they found themselves targeted from unexpected sites.

The battle waged all afternoon, each side trying to gain advantageous positions, confound the other side and annihilate them or force them to retreat.

Manuel surprised two enemy soldiers well within his sight, right below him in a hollow. They were at his mercy. Grenade in hand, then an explosion! With one jump he dropped down in a cloud of dust, smelling the gunpowder, with two dead bodies laid out before him.

At a higher altitude the rifle fire was intensifying, and Manuel realized he had separated from his *compañeros* and was confined to that hollow. It would be hard getting out. He looked at the fallen bodies, one of them face down so he couldn't see his features. The other had landed on his back, his chest bloody, his shirt decorated with fascist emblems and Franco's photo, his face untroubled, adolescent, with soft, fair skin, and luminous blue eyes that, even though he was dead, stared reverently up to the sky.

More than ousting himself from that hole he had fallen into and getting back to the fight, he needed to get out because he couldn't bear that face, so young, so calm, so eager to excuse all the fascist arrogance and hate.

He hurled himself out, jumping over ravines and mountain ledges, crawling like a cobra, hid and ran. And when he finally caught sight of his brigade's line, he saw that to reach it he would have to cross the path of fire.

He didn't hesitate, he bolted. His *compañeros* saw him and sustained fire on the enemy. Just as he approached the sacks of earth, one out of the storm of flying bullets hit him and sent him to the ground.

8

Wounded once again, this time in the leg, he returned to the field hospital. They extracted the bullet, sewed up the wound, bandaged him up and loaned him a crutch for support. "You can go home," the doctor told him, "but we're not letting you go back to the front until we take out your stitches."

At the house, as always, Madrecita took good care of him. The lack of news from her daughter threw an uneasy pall over the house. And as always, Manuel's spirit felt in conflict, between the rush to return to the front and the desire not to leave without knowing about Eulalia.

The wound had almost healed, but still the pain from it and the anxiety of not knowing gave him erratic sleep. He slept in the afternoon, and at night he stayed up late talking with Madrecita. The same thing happened every time: his head started nodding, and eventually she almost forced him to go to bed.

One night he went to his room and feel asleep. He woke up feeling a presence in the room and, opening his eyes, saw Eulalia before him. She was seated at the edge of his bed, as if she were trying not to make any noise, leaning slightly over him, quietly observing. When he opened his eyes and she saw he had seen her, she made a rapid move. She leaned over even more, her face across from his as her black hair spilled forward. They both remained for a long moment dumb with emotion. He inched back and they continued staring at one another in silence. Her eyes glistened in the semi-darkness. He wore an expression of such heightened poignancy that she had never seen in him. With her fingertips she lightly, tenderly caressed the length of his scars.

Then they embraced with a kindness that was desire and a desire that was kindness. They moved slowly, savoring the mutual discovery, unhurriedly, with every passing second adding to the sudden ecstasy of getting to know one another, naturally, honestly, spontaneously and uninhibitedly. Enraptured and impassioned, enveloped in sensuality, joy and pleasure, they reveled in a night of love.

For two whole days Madrecita, always so alive with her presence, her news and opinions, and her caring for her daughter, made herself scarce around the house. More than once, under pretext, she went out to the street for something she needed. Clearly she not only understood but approved of this love. Allowing space for the lovers, her tenderness was even deeper the more discreetly she showed it.

The farewell took place with few words. The words that could have been said were so many they had to remain unspoken. They embraced so long they could barely pull themselves apart. In a quiet voice, each of them uttered but four words.

"See you soon, Eulalia."

"See you soon, love."

They exchanged a quick kiss on the cheek.

Manuel went back to Somosierra and the Consuelo Núñez Brigade. In a few days' time, Eulalia headed off to the front at Toledo, as political commissar of the People's Army.

9

No one had to arrive in the capital needing a place to stay for Abel to make his way to Eulalia's house. He showed up from time to time and stayed to talk with Madrecita. They liked conversing with one another. For him, she was a living revelation of human beings whose fundamental motivation in life is the struggle for an ideal. For her, he was the living presence in her own house of the continuity of the struggle that she had always lived, and of her feeling that amidst the turbulence of war she could protect and save the life of one who might as well have been her own son. Truly as though he were her own son.

One day she asked him a favor. "The next time you come, come earlier. I want to give you some *churros* for breakfast."

Abel didn't disappoint. He came earlier. For each of them, it was not a mere gesture but rather something greater, profound and important.

Madrecita never took her eyes off Abel as he was eating her *churros*. When he finished, she said, slowly and simply, "Antón and Manolo also liked my *churros*."

The war dragged on, ever more widespread, violent and terrifying, with its victories and defeats, offensives and retreats. It had its moments of daring advances and other moments of imminent danger of devastating loss. At the beginning of November the government moved to Valencia, and the fascists arrived at the gates of Madrid in a powerful mobilization.

At the Casa de Campo, quite near Eulalia's house, with the people in arms and with new military units, new commanders emerged. Well-known Communists fell there. That's where Buenaventura Durruti fell, the Catalonian anarchist leader. Madrid, capital of the Republic, was subjected to terrorizing aerial bombardment. Madrid, the symbol of heroic antifascist resistance, repelled the enemy.

All over Spain, with the military intervention of Germany and Italy on one side and the growing solidarity with the Republic, the civil war took on the shape of an international war.

Certain fronts became famous—for the violence of the battle, the uncertainty of the outcome, the impact of the results, and the deeds of the combatants. Among others, Rubio was cited as one example of a remarkable commander.

The war went on and on, more cruel with each passing month, and no one could predict when it would end or how.

"Abel, *hijo mío*," Madrecita told him, "whatever happens, this is and always will be your home."

10

Without advance notice a Portuguese comrade arrived in Madrid from France via Catalonia. How he got from Portugal to France no one knew and no one tried to find out. He asked for António and Manuel, and Gonzalo pointed to Abel.

The newcomer saw the very young boy and wondered if there was some mistake. "Is this him?"

"Yes, that's the *compañero*," Gonzalo confirmed.

Abel didn't take the doubtfulness badly. In fact, the newcomer's evident shock gave him a certain pleasure.

The comrade looked at him anew with greater attention. Abel looked back authoritatively. He was scrubbed and well-dressed.

"I'll take you," Abel told him.

On the way they got to talking. In Portugal they had not received news from the Portuguese comrades in Madrid for some time. Abel brought him up to date. He also mentioned other Portuguese who had shown up and integrated into Spanish units or the International Brigades.

"Don't bother asking about them. A Lopes is enlisted as López, a Domingos as Domínguez, a Rodrigues as Rodríguez."

"Any news about Huelva?"

"No, none."

They arrived at the house. Madrecita was home and opened the door, not so cautiously as before, but quickly, eager to see who it was. "Is it you?"

She was a good friend as always, but alas, disappointed. It wasn't the person she was waiting for day after day and hour by hour.

No, she didn't know anything either about the comrades. She repeated what Abel had said. António had departed for the front some months ago now, and hadn't been heard from since. Of Manuel too, little was known. One day at Guadarrama on retreat from a new fascist advance, he remained on the other side of the line in territory occupied by the enemy. No one had seen him again, neither alive nor dead.

"My sons—" She wanted to add something more, but wasn't able.

The comrade knew of the existence of the house. "And Eulalia?" he asked.

"I don't know where she is. She also marched off to the front. She's a commissar with the People's Army. I heard from her two or three times, but it's been a long time and I haven't gotten anything from her."

Suddenly she asked, "Tell me, *compañero*, are we going to lose the war?"

Before the comrade could speak, the words of Rubio, that António quoted to Abel, passed like a bolt of lightning through his mind: *The great victories of the workers and oppressed peoples were made possible because the workers and peoples fought in every case confident of victory, but without the certainty of achieving it.*

The comrade responded. The situation was difficult. Hitler and Mussolini, with Salazar's support, wanted to smash the Spanish Republic so as to have a secure rear guard in the war they were preparing to launch in all of Europe. England and France, under the farce of "non-intervention," did not fight the Nazi-fascist intervention, namely Hitler. Rather, they preferred to remain in his good graces, while pointing him onto the path of aggression against the Soviet Union.

The comrade didn't expand much further than that, and sought to sum up the conversation.

In the coming period, the world would pass through a complex and dangerous time. But the situation would be overcome. In Portugal, in the Navy, the sailors had revolted and taken over ships. Even if the revolt was crushed, it showed tremendous revolutionary potential.

Madrecita made an effort to follow what the comrade was saying, trying to convince herself that it was real.

"The struggle continues," the comrade finished, and repeated the phrase, "*A luta continua*. Here in Spain, and all over the world, fascism will end by being destroyed. That much is certain. You can believe it, comrade."

Madrecita felt the comrade spoke the truth. Yes, he was surely right in what he said. Her question, however, did not get answered. And she also didn't care for the tone of the comrade's speech. She heard speeches like that every day.

"What I wanted," she said in a barely audible whisper, "was to receive some word about my Eulalia."

Photo: Eduardo Gageiro

A short biographical note on the author
Manuel Tiago

Manuel Tiago was the pen name of Álvaro Cunhal. Edições Avante! in Lisbon, has published nine titles by Manuel Tiago: *Até amanhã, camaradas* (Until Tomorrow, Comrades), which was adapted as a Portuguese television series in 2005; *A estrela de seis pontas* (The Six-Pointed Star); *A Casa de Eulália* (The House of Eulália); *Fronteiras* (Border Crossings); *Um risco na areia* (A Line in the Sand); *Os corrécios e outros contos* (The Slackers and Other Stories); *Sala 3 e outros contos* (The 3rd Floor and Other Stories); and *Lutas e vidas* (Struggle and Life). *Cinco dias, cinco noites* (Five Days, Five Nights), adapted to film in 1996, was the first of his works of fiction to appear in English. In its continuing series of Manual Tiago books, International Publishers has so far released *Five Days, Five Nights*, *The Six-Pointed Star*, *The 3rd Floor and Other Stories of the Portuguese Resistance*, *Border Crossings*, *The Slackers and Other Stories,* and now *Eulalia's House*.

Álvaro Cunhal was born in Coimbra, Portugal, on November 9, 1913. He began his revolutionary activity as a student at the law school (Faculdade de Direito) of Lisbon. He participated in the student movement and was elected in 1934 as the student representative to the University Senate. He was a militant in the Federation of Portuguese Communist Youth (Federação da Juventude Comunista Portuguesa), and was elected its secretary-general in 1935. In that year he went underground and participated in Moscow in the Sixth International Communist Youth Congress. He joined the Portuguese Communist Party (Partido Comunista Português, PCP) in 1931.

Arrested in 1937 and 1940, and subjected to torture, he returned to political struggle as soon as he was freed after several months in prison. He participated in the reorganization of the PCP in the early 1940s. Again living clandestinely, he was a member of the party Secretariat from 1942 to 1949.

Arrested anew in 1949 and brought before a fascist court, he delivered a ringing denunciation of the fascist dictatorship and a defense of his party's program. Judged guilty, he remained for 11 years in fascist prisons, almost eight of them in complete isolation. On January 3, 1960, he escaped from the prison fortress at Peniche together with a group of brave communist militants. Once again called to the Secretariat of the Central Committee, he was elected Secretary General of the PCP in 1961.

Living abroad, in Moscow and Paris, from that time forward he participated in numerous congresses and gatherings with communist parties and other revolutionary forces in international conferences. He played a critical role in organizing worldwide support, especially within the socialist countries, for the independence movements in the far-flung Portuguese colonies in Africa.

After the downfall of the fascist dictatorship on April 25, 1974, he served as Minister without Portfolio in the first four provisional governments, and was elected as a deputy to the Constituent Assembly in 1975 and to the Assembly for the Republic in 1975, 1979, 1980, 1983, 1985 and 1987. He was a member of the Council of State from 1982 to 1992.

In accordance with the decisions made at the 14th Congress of the PCP in 1992 concerning renewal and a new structure of leadership, he stepped down as Secretary General of the PCP and was elected by the Central Committee as President of the National Council of the party.

In December 1996, the 15th Congress of the PCP eliminated the National Council of the party and its presidency. Cunhal was re-elected as a member of the Central Committee.

He was re-elected to the Central Committee at the 16th and 17th party congresses in December 2000 and November 2004 respectively.

Under his own name Cunhal published several books about politics. He was a gifted artist as well: A book of his collected drawings has appeared. In addition, he published an original translation of Shakespeare's *King Lear*.

He died at the age of 91 on June 13, 2005. His funeral in Lisbon was attended by half a million people. He had one daughter, Ana Cunhal. The Portuguese government issued a postage stamp in his memory and later, in 2021, another stamp commemorating the centennial of the PCP to which he had devoted his life.

Photo: Fernando Pereira

About the Translator

ERIC A. Gordon, a Los Angeles resident since 1990, is a native of New Haven, Connecticut. His undergraduate degree is from Yale University, where he majored in Latin American Studies. He studied Spanish five years and Portuguese two years. He also took a summer residency in Portuguese at New York University. He went on to Tulane University, where he continued studying Portuguese and wrote a master's thesis on the opera in Rio de Janeiro in the 19th century, using original sources uncovered in the Arquivo Nacional. He earned a doctorate in history, also from Tulane, writing his dissertation about the anarchist movement in Brazil in the pre-World War I era. He also studied Portuguese language and culture under a Gulbenkian Foundation fellowship in Lisbon.

International Publishers initiated its Manuel Tiago series in 2020 with Gordon's translation of *Five Days, Five Nights*, followed by *The Six-Pointed Star, The 3rd Floor and Other Stories of the Portuguese Resistance, Border Crossings, The Slackers and Other Stories,* and now *Eulalia's House*. When complete, the series will comprise all nine works of fiction by Álvaro Cunhal, each appearing for the first time in English.

Gordon is the author of *Mark the Music: The Life and Work of Marc Blitzstein*, and co-author of *Ballad of an American: The Autobiography of Earl Robinson*. A memoir in short story form that he translated from Portuguese, *Waving to the Train and Other Stories*, by Hadasa Cytrynowicz, appeared in 2013 from Blue Thread Press. In 2015 he executive produced the compact disk *City of the Future: Yiddish Songs from the Former Soviet Union*, a collection of songs composed in 1931 by Samuel Polonski to the lyrics of major Soviet Yiddish poets. He is the author of a currently unpublished political autobiography.

From 1995 to 2010, Gordon was Director of the Workers Circle/ Arbeter Ring in Southern California. He previously worked at Social and Public Art Resource Center, helping to produce murals all around the city of Los Angeles, which gave him the experience to commission a mural at the Workers Circle building. He was Southern California Chapter Chair of the National Writers Union (Local

1981 UAW/AFL-CIO) for two terms. He has written for dozens of local, national, and international publications, mostly about art, music, culture, and politics. From 2014 onward, he has been a staff writer and editor for *People's World* online newspaper.

From 2006-09 Gordon took coursework toward certification as a Secular Jewish Leader, referred to in Yiddish as a *vegvayzer*. Upon graduation, he became a legal officiant certified to conduct weddings and other ceremonial functions, a role equivalent in law to a minister, priest, or rabbi. He has a similar endorsement as a Humanist celebrant for people of any background. For five years he served as a Deputy Commissioner of Civil Marriage for the County of Los Angeles, where he conducted 1500 marriages.

Eric Gordon can be contacted at ericarthurgo@gmail.com.

Questions to Ponder and Discuss

At the very end, the Portuguese comrade sums up the reasons and the character of the war. It's clear he holds the Western democracies at fault for their failure to intervene on the Republican side. Elsewhere in the book as well there are discussions about foreign policy, especially on the British and French sides. Does that analysis conform to your overall understanding of the Spanish Civil War, or do you see it perhaps from another angle?

Now that this novel is appearing for the first time in English, did you stop to think about what the role of the United States and other English-speaking countries was during this period?

Did Rubio's success as a military commander come as a surprise to you, or did you notice signs of it earlier in the book?

António steals a peasant's shoes at gunpoint. Did he have no other alternative?

The author does not mention it again, but do you think that the nurse Celia's rejection of António had anything to do with his reassessment of his own masculinity and the life-changing decision he comes to toward the end? Did he, perhaps not so subconsciously, wish to die for the cause to prove he was not a coward?

How well do you feel the author represented women in this story?

Were you affected by the discussion about "confidence" versus "certainty?"

For you as a reader, did the author adequately identify the social classes and interests within Spain that supported fascism? And those that supported the Republic?

Did he fairly represent some of the other factions on the Republican side apart from the Communists?

Related to the above questions, why do you think the author omitted any reference to the strong influence of the Catholic Church as a force opposing the Republic?

Tiago underlines many times the spontaneity of the people, and how they came together, much of the time leaderless, to solve their problems. The creation of the field hospital is the prime example, but the battlefield itself is perhaps an even more powerful example. Do you believe he is stating the case for a kind of homemade, naturally evolving communism? Don't forget, many of the anarchists and syndicalists at the time saw the civil war as not so much defending a parliamentary Republic but of making a Revolution.

How do you see The Comrade, the nameless Party leader whom António and Manuel report to? Who is he exactly? He's not a public figure at all, so do you think it's possible he is the same Portuguese—also nameless—"comrade" at the end, who tellingly comes to Madrid from Portugal to France through Catalonia, exactly the reverse course The Comrade took to leave Spain? He asks, "Is this him?" when he's introduced to Abel, obviously knowing it's not António but not saying so. Was he just being evasive so as not to reveal his identity?

How do you see António's relationship with The Comrade? Clearly they are not "equals," and António often chafes at the presumption that he is expected to follow the advice (perhaps better, orders?) of the comrade more senior in rank. In the clear, unsentimental light of Party thinking, António sometimes feels unsupported for the great sacrifices he makes. In the end and on his own, António hands over his functions to Abel and goes his own way, disagreeing with his Party comrades. His attitude toward The Comrade may be only part of his predicament—maybe he has issues with the more basic concept of "the interests of the party." Your thoughts?

How do you interpret the presence of men like Barata and Stockler, as well as the three members of the Hotel Berne Group, in the story?

Unlike a short story for the most part, the breadth and depth of the novel format permit the author a much deeper examination of people and how they change over time. What characters undergo personal transformations and how would you describe them?

Do you come away from this novel with a clearer understanding of why people flocked to Spain from all over the world to defend the Spanish Republic even at the risk of their own lives?

Is there any struggle in your own life experience that compares to the level of principled devotion these characters such as António, Renato, Manuel, Eulalia, Isabel, Madrecita and so many others demonstrated in Spain?

If you could say anything, or ask any question to the author, what would it be?

Forthcoming from International Publishers: The next book in the complete fiction of Manuel Tiago

A Line in the Sand

(Um risco na areia)

Chapter 1

The old warehouse attached to the little residence now served as the reception room of the *Centro de Trabalho*—the Party Center—of Santa Efigénia Parish. That September day, just after noon, hundreds of comrades were getting ready for a demonstration.

So many people being there made it hard to move about. In that ample space, with all the excited coming and going, you couldn't avoid bumping into people. Different groups flashed their brightly colored flags and banners as they rehearsed their slogans. Near the outside door laborers were waiting, dressed in their work clothes. Everyone had the anticipatory mood of people ready to step forth.

Some of the young folks were standing stock still, impatient with waiting. A young woman proudly gripped a huge red banner. The young people stood in a compact unit poised to join the demonstration parade.

Among them, one looked out of place, with no flag, no banner, with no image of Lenin or Che Guevara on his shirt, and not even the emblem of the Communist Youth. He wore just a plain white shirt and ordinary pants. Nevertheless, it was clear that the others accepted him as he was. They knew he was from far away, and that by night he wandered the streets watching the passing scene. And, strangely enough, he could predict the rise of dangerous situations and would intervene at the right places at the right times.

Beyond the group, a very young woman, a girl really, meandered through the room, checking in with and helping various clusters of demonstrators.

One of the other young women watched her, smiling. "Isa doesn't want to have anything to do with us. She thinks she's a grown woman already."

"You have a sharp tongue, Berta," someone beside her observed.

"That's what's missing with you, my friend," Berta replied.

From time to time, the door leading from the house into the reception hall opened, and a comrade came out. He assembled various groupings and gave everyone instructions. He was the director and organizer of the march. A singular character of a certain age, with white hair and a pleasant face, he walked with some difficulty, dragging one leg behind him in grotesque jerky movements. He spoke with different people and then disappeared back through the door to the inside.

"David isn't getting better—after getting out of prison and then that fall that broke his leg and foot," one comrade said.

"It's a shame," another commented, "he was the best of them all."

Alternating with David, a young woman whom everybody knew, also came out from the inside at a quick, energetic pace, giving instructions. It was Matilde, a teacher from a school in the old city. She was the first one to single out the house where they would install the Party Center.

At the improvised bar, Joaquina, working alone, was deluged by people asking to be served. Cremilde, her colleague at the bar, hadn't shown up—and it wasn't only that day. She frequently failed to show up or arrived late. The comrades noticed, and came to their own, different conclusions: That she had her own life. That it wasn't fair to leave all the work to Joaquina. That such lack of discipline shouldn't be allowed.

On the other hand, it should be said that when she did come and work at the bar, she was respected and liked. Unlike Joaquina, she spoke in a calm, quiet voice, and her moves were more deliberate. But she tended the bar as well and as quickly as her companion.

Joaquina often found herself at loose ends tending to so many comrades. So whenever anyone cut ahead of the others and tried to order, she promptly responded in her accent from Alentejo, "First come, first served, comrade!"

And if they still insisted, she answered, "If you don't want to wait, then get out of the way."

"That Joaquina is a terror! She's got an answer to everything," people said—but not in anger, more out of amusement.

In the midst of such a crush of comrades, a loud voice called their attention. One group, shouting, "*Viva! Viva!*," tried to start off the march, unfurling and waving their two big red flags. Then the speaker summoned their attention. The moment had not yet come.

Out of the group of young people, one voice could be heard. "It's time we left already." It was Berta.

Two unfamiliar men came in from the street, making their way through the crowd. They spoke in the familiar terms of fellow Party members. "Who's in charge of the Center?" they asked.

They crossed through the mass of people, and David led them into an office where Marco also was waiting. And they left shortly.

Weird. They arrived and left just like that, and no one knew why or for what.

Before long, Marco appeared, upright and serious as always. People opened up his passageway to the packed bar, and he asked for a coffee. Some of the comrades respectfully yielded their place at the counter.

Everyone, of course, wished to ask what those two unknown comrades wanted. "Any news, Marco?" someone asked.

He responded modestly and briefly. "What we have been saying has been confirmed. A flyer is being circulated by the thousands all over the country announcing a march on Lisbon on the 28th by the so-called 'silent majority.'" So it was confirmed that this dangerous development would take place in two weeks' time.

As if oblivious to this news, the crowd started showing signs of impatience.

"What are we still doing here? It's time to step off," Berta repeated loudly, making herself heard throughout the hall.

With everything set, the final signal to march was given. The demonstration headed out to the Ministry of Labor.

Once the signal came, Nelo asked the young man with no insignias, "Are you ready, Zé Manuel?"

The mass that had been standing and waiting up to that point, now shot out like a hurricane, almost in military formation.

Nelo pushed through the others, and when Berta stumbled and fell back a few paces, he turned around. "Berta! Berta! You're always behind."

Always was not true, but it did happen that time.

The marchers of Santa Efigénia paraded proudly through the streets, exalted by what they had succeeded in organizing. They believed they would lend a unique significance and energy to this mass public demonstration. But as they approached, they were surprised to see other organized groups, some with considerably more people, marching toward the same location. When they got there it was an extraordinary shock. Every demonstration from the different parishes, from workplaces, from unions, merged into one great ocean of demonstrators.

"Over a hundred thousand," said the newspapers, with demands from the labor movement and against the reactionaries.

But would these demonstrations lead the right wing to hold off on this new coup they had openly announced?

Lightning Source UK Ltd.
Milton Keynes UK
UKHW010901070922
408363UK00011B/124